A DROP IN THE POTION

A SPELLBOUND PARANORMAL COZY MYSTERY, BOOK 8

ANNABEL CHASE

RED PALM PRESS LLC

A Drop in the Potion

A Spellbound Paranormal Cozy Mystery, Book 8

By Annabel Chase

Sign up for my newsletter here http://eepurl.com/ctYNzf and or like me on Facebook **so you can find out about new releases**.

Copyright © 2017 Red Palm Press LLC

Cover Design by Alchemy

❀ Created with Vellum

CHAPTER 1

"Excellent," Begonia said as we entered the academy classroom. "Substitute today."

Ginger stood at the front of the classroom, one eye trained on the clock. "Have a seat, witches, and we'll get started. Lady Weatherby and Professor Holmes are running late in a coven meeting, so they've asked me to cover your class today."

"Do we need to stick to the normal lesson plan?" Laurel asked.

Ginger flipped her red hair over her shoulder. "Just because I'm a substitute doesn't mean we can ditch the curriculum."

"Can we at least modify it today?" Sophie asked. "Combine something useful with something fun?"

Ginger seemed prepared to consider the idea. "What do you have in mind?"

"We want to learn to fight like the Amazons in Wonder Woman," Sophie said.

Ginger squinted at her. "What's Wonder Woman?"

Sophie's cheeks turned pink. "Nothing. Did I say Wonder Woman?" She didn't want to reveal that the magic mirror in the secret lair provided endless hours of cinematic entertainment from the human world. "I meant an Amazon like Juliet Montlake."

"The only thing I've seen Juliet Montlake fight over is a parking spot near the Wish Market," Ginger replied. She tapped her wand in the palm of her hand. "So you want to learn some fighting moves, huh? Is that the bottom line?"

Five heads bobbed up and down.

"I suppose I could deviate a smidge from the lesson plan." Ginger cocked her red head, thinking. "You never know when you're going to need good attack moves."

"It's Spellbound," Millie said. "It can happen at any moment."

"Oh, come on," Ginger objected. "It's not that dangerous here."

"We have murders, magical crimes, theft, abuse of power." Millie ticked them off on her fingers. "We're practically an evil enclave."

Ginger laughed. "Don't you think you might be exaggerating just a little bit?"

"Teach us something cool," Laurel said. "Something I can use to threaten my brothers when they're annoying."

Ginger held up an index finger. "That I can assist with." She pointed her wand at the adjacent wall and said, "A bone to its marrow/shoot me an arrow."

An arrow shot from the tip of her wand just as Sedgwick decided to fly in through the open door and join the class. He swooped out of the way in the nick of time. The arrow whizzed past him, the point stuck firmly in the wall.

I whistled. "You'd give Robin Hood a run for his money." I paused. "Or a run for the rich people's money he stole."

Gee, don't be concerned on my account, Sedgwick said from

his perch on a nearby shelf. *My feathers are practically a suit of armor.*

She missed, didn't she? I glared at him. *And if you'd been on time that would never have happened.*

And if you didn't take so long in the bathroom, I'd have been on time, Sedgwick argued.

You're ridiculous, I replied. *You're an owl. You don't need the bathroom.*

"What else can you do?" Begonia asked the teacher, her blue eyes shining.

"Emma, why don't you stand beneath the shelf where Sedgwick is?" Ginger said.

I hesitated. "Is this going to be a William Tell situation? Do I need an apple?" I was fairly certain my sorcery skills could manifest an apple.

"I don't know who William Tell is," Ginger said, and readied her wand for another spell.

I stood underneath the shelf and waited. To my surprise, she took aim at Sedgwick rather than me.

"River wide, ocean deep/this dart will make you fall asleep."

A tranquilizer dart shot from the end of her wand and landed directly in Sedgwick's belly. I knew where it hit without looking because I felt a shadow of my familiar's pain. There was no time to react, though, because Sedgwick teetered off the edge of the shelf and plummeted toward the floor. I reached out and caught him before he was a pile of flattened feathers.

"He could've been hurt," I said, glaring at Ginger. I didn't care that she was in charge of today's class. The only one allowed to abuse my cranky owl was *me*.

"No, he couldn't have been," she replied matter-of-factly. "Why do you think I asked you to stand there?"

I glanced at the unconscious owl in my arms. "How long will he be out for?"

"A while," Ginger replied. "I would think it's less distracting for you to have him sleeping."

"Not if I'm worrying about him," I said. "Can you wake him up?"

Ginger pointed her wand at Sedgwick. "No more sleep to take/make this owl awake."

Sedgwick's large owl eyes popped open, startling me. I jumped back and he flew out my arms, indignant.

Why did I bother showing up for your class? he grumbled, and flew back to the safety of the shelf.

"What else can shoot out of a wand?" Laurel asked. Despite my owl's trauma, she clearly was enjoying every moment of today's lesson.

"We already know how to use our wands to create light and water," Millie said, ever the Hermione of our little group.

"Sometimes I use mine as a laser pointer," Begonia said. "My familiar loves to chase the light around the floor. We should get Chairman Meow down here to experiment with it."

"A laser pointer isn't very handy as a means of attack, though, is it?" Millie said snidely. "Unless you're planning to bore someone to death with a presentation."

A slow smile spread across Ginger's pretty face. "I've got one." She aimed her wand at the blinds first, dropping them down. Then she dimmed the fey lanterns in the classroom so that it was pitch dark.

"I can't see," Millie complained. "How can I take notes on the spell?"

I can see fine, Sedgwick gloated.

Save your superiority. Millie can't hear you, I said.

Sedgwick ruffled his feathers in annoyance. *Ooh, I like what she's about to...*

4

Before he could finish, light exploded in the room, blinding all of us.

"My eyes," Millie cried, covering her face.

"I bet that's not the kind of light you meant," Sophie whispered to Millie.

By the time my eyes adjusted to the sudden change, Ginger managed to restore normal light to the classroom.

"I didn't hear the spell because I was too busy protecting myself from blindness," Millie complained. "Can you repeat it so I can write it down?"

Ginger suppressed a smile. "I said it quietly. I'm not sure I should share that one yet. It's very powerful and I've already shown you more than I should have."

"Please, Ginger," Laurel said. "What if we're trapped in a cave and it's the only way to frighten the spiders away?"

"Spiders?" Begonia queried with a shiver. "Why would we be trapped in a cave with spiders?"

Ginger's shoulders relaxed. "Okay, fine. But do *not* share this with anyone or use it inappropriately. Got it?"

We all nodded.

"Wand reload/light explode." Ginger shrugged. "That's it. Of course, you need to focus your will very carefully. Otherwise, you could end up exploding the wand. Then you'd be defenseless against the spiders."

"Ugh. Spiders," Begonia repeated and hugged herself.

"You do realize there are no actual spiders," Millie snapped. "This is all hypothetical."

Laurel raised her hand. "Can we try now?"

Ginger chewed her lip. "I don't know, Laurel. It was one thing to show you…"

"At least let Emma try," Sophie said. "She's supposed to do more advanced work now anyway."

That was true. I'd been training with Lady Weatherby and Agnes privately on top of the remedial witch classes. They wanted to make sure my sorceress powers didn't run amok and destroy everything in their path.

"Emma, are you interested?" Ginger asked.

I glanced at my friends, who nodded encouragingly. "I guess I am."

Ginger waved me forward. "Then let's go."

I stepped up to the front of the classroom clutching my light blue wand, Tiffany. "Arrow first?"

Ginger shrugged. "Whatever flies your broomstick."

"Nothing," Millie snickered. "She's terrible on a broomstick."

"You're in quite a mood today, Millie," Ginger said, pinning Millie with a hard stare. "Is there anything you need to discuss with me after class?"

Millie's gaze dropped to the table in front of her. "No, miss," she mumbled.

I pointed my wand at the adjacent wall and repeated Ginger's spell. An arrow shot from the end of the wand and narrowly missed one of the fey light sconces.

"Oops," I said. "I need better aim."

"It takes time and patience," Ginger said. "Like everything to do with magic. How about the dart?"

Try the far wall this time, Sedgwick urged, unwilling to participate again.

I focused my will and pointed my wand well over the girls' heads. "From the wand of Emma Hart/shoot me a dart."

"Cute," Ginger said.

The wand released a tranquilizer dart on command. Unfortunately, Lady Weatherby chose that particular moment to check on the status of our lesson. She stepped through the open doorway, her black cloak billowing around her.

I opened my mouth to stop the spell, but it was too late. The dart landed squarely in her chest. She glanced down briefly to see the red tassels of the dart dangling from her dress before she slumped to the floor.

My wand shook in my hand as I lowered it. Slowly, I turned my head to look at Ginger. "Did she see it was me?"

Ginger heaved a sigh. "I don't think so."

"Let's never tell her, okay?" I pleaded.

The other girls crowded around the head of the coven.

"Should we wake her?" Millie asked, giving the witch's leg a hesitant nudge with her toe.

Begonia balled her fists in a nervous gesture. "I think Ginger should do it once we've gone."

"Good idea," Sophie added. "Class is over now anyway, right?"

We all looked expectantly at Ginger.

"Oh, fine," Ginger said. "I suppose this is my fault anyway. I should have stuck to the original plan."

Sedgwick swooped over our heads and flew out the door. *I'm not getting caught up in any of this mess. See you at home, loser.*

"See you later, fair feather friend," I called with a sarcastic wave.

"Secret lair at eight?" Sophie asked, stepping over a section of Lady Weatherby's cloak.

"I'll be there," Millie said.

"I'm meeting Demetrius for dinner, but I'll come after," Begonia said.

"Demetrius again?" Sophie queried. "You two had dinner earlier this week."

"I think you'll find they have dinner every night," Laurel said. "Just not necessarily with each other."

Ginger placed her hands on her hips. "Witches, if you don't want Lady Weatherby to wake up and see you all staring down at her, I highly suggest you get a move on."

She didn't need to say it twice. We filed out through the

doorway, careful not to trip over Lady Weatherby's crumpled body.

"Good luck," I called over my shoulder, and ran out of the building as fast as I could.

CHAPTER 2

"I THINK I'm going to call my tattoo business Spelled Ink," Begonia announced.

We'd gathered in the secret lair that evening. It was a good thing we'd already made plans to do so because rumor had it that Lady Weatherby had awoken from her unexpected nap in a very foul mood.

"I don't get it," Millie said.

"It's a play on words," Laurel explained. "There's spilled ink but also inc. like incorporated and spelled instead of spilled because of magic."

Millie seemed unimpressed.

"Personally, I love the name," Sophie said. "The business is going to be a lot of work, though. Are you sure you're up for it?"

"Demetrius said he would help me set it up," Begonia replied.

Millie glowered. "Is that how it's going to be now? Same as with Claude. A boyfriend comes along and your coven sisters are stale bread?"

Begonia looked genuinely hurt. "How can you say that? You girls will always be more important to me. It's just that Demetrius has a lot of experience in business and he offered to help. I would be silly to turn it down."

"Whatever," Millie grumbled.

Begonia fingered the ideal beauty necklace wrapped around the neck of one of the voodoo dolls. "So should this doll look like the most beautiful doll in the world to me now?"

Millie snatched the doll out of her hand. "I'm still perfecting the spell. Genius can't be rushed."

"It seemed to work well enough on us," Laurel said. "Not so sure what the point would be for inanimate objects."

Millie removed the necklace from the doll and handed it to Begonia. "Here. You can mess around with it if you want. I'm working on another project right now anyway. I'm like a shark. If I stagnate, I die."

I stifled a laugh. Millie was like a shark, but not for the reasons she seemed to think.

"It's getting late. Are we going to watch a movie?" I asked. "Because I promised Daniel I'd be home early."

Millie rolled her eyes. "Oh, look. Here's another one forfeiting her sisters for a guy."

"It isn't because I prefer Daniel's company over yours," I said, though to some degree it was. "It's because Gareth and Magpie are stretched to the limit with Daniel's appearances. I'm afraid they're going to stage a coup if I'm not there to intervene."

"I can understand it from Gareth's point of view," Sophie said. "And Magpie's for that matter. It was one thing for you to move in and take over. Daniel is an angel. He can't help but rattle a vampire and his demon cat."

"Magpie isn't a demon cat," I said. Most of the time.

"You've been awfully quiet, Laurel. What are you doing over there?"

Laurel sat at the small table, with a pile of open books in front of her. In the stack, I noticed the old grimoire that she'd discovered in the coven library.

"I've been working on a reveal spell so I can read my sister's journal," Laurel explained. "She's been taunting me with its contents for months. I'm determined to figure out a way to read it."

Millie's eyes lit up. "I can help you with that. I used one on my sister's journal last year. I knew she borrowed my other sister's broomstick and damaged it, but she refused to own up to it. She tried to play me. I knew she'd boast about it in her journal."

"And did she?" Begonia asked.

Millie folded her arms smugly. "Of course she did. I know my sister well. I did the reveal spell and was able to show my parents the evidence that it wasn't me. My sister was punished for a fortnight." She sighed. "Sweet justice."

Laurel held up the parchment for inspection. "Then I would love it if you'd take a look at my spell and tell me if this seems accurate to you."

Millie plucked the paper from Laurel's fingers and examined the contents. She paced the lair, muttering the words under her breath. "I think you're missing a line here." She tapped a spot on the page. "Other than that, it looks good."

"What do you think I should add?" Laurel asked.

Millie glanced around the room. "Where's a quill?" Before anyone could answer, she spotted one on the coffee table. She kneeled on the floor and scribbled in the missing line. Then she returned the sheet to Laurel. "Try this."

Laurel reviewed the new addition. "Oh, of course. Good thinking."

11

"Do you actually have her journal?" I asked.

Laurel shook her head. "She has a protective spell around it. I'm able to read it where it is, but if I try to move it, an alarm will go off."

"Can't you do it when she's not home?" Sophie asked. "That way it doesn't matter if an alarm goes off."

Laurel looked up at us. "The alarm isn't to alert her. It's triggered to do something to the wannabe thief. I'm not risking a new nose or frog legs for this."

"So how will you know if your spell works?" I asked. "Did you bring something to practice on?"

"I have a book from the library that includes concealment spells and examples of how they work." She began to riffle through the pile of books on the table. "I thought I would practice my spell on the examples in the book to see if it works."

I ruffled Laurel's hair. "You're so clever. You're going to be the smartest witch in the coven someday."

Begonia beamed at the youngest member of the remedial witch class. "I think she already is."

Laurel pulled a book from the middle of the stack and opened it to a marked page. "This is one of the cloaked samples."

We watched as she performed her spell on the page. The words shimmered before dissolving, leaving an image of a cauldron in its place.

"Wow," Sophie said. "That's so cool."

"Operation Sister's Journal is in full effect," Laurel said proudly.

"Have you found anything interesting in the old grimoire?" I asked, nudging the book on the table. "I see you've been tackling that, too."

Laurel nodded and swapped the books so that the

grimoire was open in front of her. "There's something odd about this page. It's been bothering me, but I can't put my finger on it."

I went to peer over her shoulder. "What's weird about it?" To the untrained eye, it looked like just another yellowed page in an ancient grimoire.

Laurel touched the inner binding. "There are a couple of issues. One is the binding here is slightly different from the other pages in the book. It almost looks like it was sealed in later."

"Like an updated edition?" I queried.

"I don't know," she replied. "The middle of the book is a funny place to add an update."

"Maybe they realized that they were missing a page after they finished putting it together," I suggested. "They had no choice but to go back in and add it later." It wasn't like they had computers and could print the whole thing again.

"And what?" Laurel asked. "They used magic to seal it in?"

"Why not?" I read the words on the page, but they seemed unremarkable to me. "Is there anything significant?"

Laurel frowned. "No, and that's one of the things that's bothering me. It's the least inconsequential page in the entire grimoire. The spells are far less sophisticated on this page than on page one. It doesn't make sense."

The other witches gathered closer for a better glimpse of the page.

"What kind of spells?" Sophie asked. "Anything we want to learn?"

"That's my point," Laurel said. "I think we've learned these already. There's a light spell and a color change spell. What's the point of having these in the middle of an ancient grimoire?"

Millie ran a finger down the page. "I agree. Spells like

these belong at the beginning. Maybe they were in the beginning of the book and had fallen out at some point, and someone sealed them back in the wrong spot."

Laurel chewed her lip. "That's a possibility. Though it should have been obvious where the page actually belonged."

"Sometimes I find it helps if I give my mind a break and do something else," I said. "When I used to practice law, sometimes ideas will come to me at the strangest times, like I wrote when I was in the shower or driving my car."

"You say that like you don't practice law now," Sophie said. "You're the town defense attorney."

"That's true," I said. "It's been slow lately, though."

"I would think that's a good thing," Millie said. "We want less crime in Spellbound."

"Yes, it is. And I've been so busy with other matters, it isn't like I need the work."

Begonia remained focused on the mysterious page. "Maybe we're missing something. Maybe there's another spell hidden within these spells. Something dangerous that only a more experienced witch could see."

Laurel brightened. "I like that idea. Maybe each letter is a code for another letter." She began to pore over each word with greater care.

"You know what?" Millie said, scrutinizing the page. "Even the ink looks different from the other pages you've shown me."

Laurel flipped back a couple of pages.

"Millie's right," I said. "It's not the same ink. The color is slightly off."

A faint smile touched Laurel's lips. "I have an idea."

"Yes, but is it a good one?" Millie challenged.

"We'll find out in a second." Laurel held up her wand and performed the reveal spell that she'd created for her sister's journal. Like in the other book, the words shimmered before dissolving.

There was a collective gasp.

"Spell's bells, Laurel," Begonia cried. "What happened to the page in the grimoire? It's got funny markings all over it now."

Begonia was right. The spells had been replaced by unfamiliar stick marks.

Laurel stared in awe at the page. "They're runes."

"Runes?" I echoed. "What do they mean?" They reminded me of Egyptian hieroglyphics but without any rounded edges.

Laurel lifted the book and held the page closer to examine it. "I have no idea, but we have to find out."

"So there was a concealment spell on the page?" Millie asked.

"That explains why the page didn't seem quite right," Sophie said.

"Someone took pains to hide it in an old grimoire," Laurel said. "I bet whoever did this wanted it to blend, but not so much that they couldn't find it later if they needed it."

"This is the most exciting thing that's happened in the secret lair in ages," Begonia said, clapping giddily.

Millie fixed her with a hard stare. "Really? Let's review. We've turned Emma invisible, practiced magic on voodoo dolls, developed our own advanced spells, but a concealed page in a dusty, old book is the highlight in your mind?"

Begonia's expression crumbled. "Well, it has the potential to be exciting. I suppose it depends on *what* is being concealed."

"Do you recognize any of those runes, Laurel?" Sophie asked.

Laurel nodded. "A couple. I'll have to start a decoding

sheet. Match the rune to its meaning and try to piece it all together like a puzzle."

"That'll keep you busy," Millie said. "Your sister's journal will seem far less important now."

Laurel touched the markings on the page. "You may have to deliver my meals here. I won't want to go home until I've cracked the code."

"Don't go all *A Beautiful Mind* on me," I said. "We need you sane, Laurel."

Millie arched an eyebrow. "Movie reference?"

"Of course," I replied. "We'll magic mirror it one of these days. It's a good one." I studied the runes over Laurel's shoulder. "Do we have any rune experts in the coven?"

"Possibly, but it would have to be someone we trust not to run off with it to Lady Weatherby," Millie said. "Can you think of anyone who fits that description?"

Actually, I could.

"Is there a way to make a copy of the page?" I asked. Where was a photocopier when I needed one? Then again, if my experience in the human world was anything to go on, using a copier would result in a paper jam and the destruction of the original. Not ideal.

"What about your spell?" Millie asked. "The one you invented where the quill writes out what you want?"

I smacked my forehead. "Millie, that's genius." I performed my spell using Laurel's quill and a spare piece of paper. I double-checked to make sure that each rune was copied exactly as it appeared on the page.

"What will you do with the copy?" Laurel asked.

"I'll let you know once I've done it," I said. "In the meantime, you keep working on it. Between the two of us, we may just figure it out."

"Okay, now who wants to volunteer for one of my new tattoos?" Begonia asked.

"I thought you were concentrating on the business formation," Sophie said.

Begonia shrugged. "No point in forming a business if I don't have enough inventory to interest buyers."

"And this is the fun part, I imagine," I said.

Begonia winked at me. "I'll let you know once I've done it."

CHAPTER 3

"WHERE'S LADY WEATHERBY?" I asked, surveying the activities room. I'd been practicing sorcery weekly with the mother-daughter magical duo, but only Agnes was here today.

"You've got to stop referring to her as Lady Weatherby to me," Agnes said. "She's Jacinda Ruth."

"Not to me," I said. And no way was I going to risk Lady Weatherby overhearing me call her Jacinda Ruth. She'd probably hex me in retaliation.

"She left word with the fairy in reception that she needed to attend to an administrative matter." Agnes clucked her tongue. "That girl takes everything so seriously. Always did."

"That *girl* is the head of the coven," I said. "Taking the role seriously is a good quality."

Agnes's eyes glinted in the artificial light of the care home. "I heard you took her out with a tranquilizer dart."

I knew word would get around, despite Ginger's promise. "It was an accident."

She cackled. "Sure it was. Where's your weapon now?" She wiggled her fingers and I handed over my wand. "You used a concealment spell?"

"Yes, I concealed it in my cloak and no one frisked me," I said. "I gave reception a fake wand to hold for me."

Agnes tapped her temple. "Good thinking, my dear. So what are we working on today?"

"I'd like to keep working on the manifestation spell," I said. "I really want to try to bring my mother's letters to Spellbound."

During a recent dream, I encountered a box in my grandparents' converted barn that contained at least twenty-seven letters from my biological mother. I didn't have time to read the letters before I was sucked out of the dream, but if I could bring the letters here through a manifestation spell, then I could read them at my leisure. Otherwise, I would have to keep going back into the dream state and seeing whether I could read them all before I woke up. I could try a dream spell, but that method would take longer and be more dangerous. There was also a chance that I wouldn't get back to the same place in the dream. Perfecting the manifestation spell seemed to be the smarter play.

The elderly witch studied me. "Have you considered the possibility that the letters won't say what you want them to say?"

"What do you mean? I don't have any expectations."

Agnes scratched the wart on her chin. "Are you sure about that?"

"Of course. I don't know anything about her." Especially since I'd only just learned of her existence.

"You believe these letters will contain information about why she left you," Agnes said. "What if they don't? Or what if they do, but the reasons aren't what you hope they are? Are you prepared to be disappointed?"

To be honest, I hadn't considered that possibility. Agnes was right. Deep down, I was convinced the letters would reveal my mother's motives for abandoning me, and offer clues to my adoptive mother's death.

"Whatever the reality is, I need to know the truth, no matter how painful. If there's a chance that I can understand my past, then I need to take it."

Agnes nodded. "And I'll support you, whatever you decide. Let me know and I'll have a bottle of Goddess Bounty ready for both of us."

"Why for both of us?" I queried. "I'm the one who would be taking an emotional risk."

"Watching you emote will be reason enough for me," Agnes replied.

"Fair enough," I said. "Should we get started?"

"We have to," she replied. "I have a game of tiddlywinks in an hour."

"Tiddlywinks?" I repeated. "Isn't that a children's game?"

Agnes smiled, revealing her crooked teeth. "Not the way we play it."

I groaned. No more questions about tiddlywinks.

Using my wand, Agnes set to work preparing a protection spell around the room. I watched her carefully, trying to pick up tidbits in case I ever needed to create a protective barrier by myself. Lady Weatherby wanted me to take things slowly, so she was perpetuating the 'one spell at a time rule' during these private lessons. Since I was focused on the manifestation spell, I was discouraged from trying any protection spells.

"Okay, buttercup. You know the drill," Agnes said, handing over my wand. "Focus your will and let's get a move on. The clock is ticking."

I sat in the middle of the circle in a cross-legged position. I wasn't flexible enough to remain in this position for very long. Last week I'd gotten a cramp in my foot and had to jump up mid-spell, yelping in pain. Lady Weatherby and

Agnes thought that something had gone horribly wrong with the spell. I had to explain to them that something had gone horribly wrong with my body instead. Lady Weatherby made the sensible suggestion that I join the coven yoga class. I didn't have the heart to tell her that yoga and I were inherently incompatible.

I closed my eyes and focused my will, pulling the magic within me. I pictured myself in my grandparents' barn, opening the box with the letters. I imagined touching the symbol of the oval wreath on the backs of the letters.

I felt something solid in my hand, so I opened my eyes and stared into my lap. "These aren't the letters." I couldn't keep the disappointment for my voice.

Agnes glanced at the papers. "Are you sure? Maybe they just don't look the way you remember them from the dream."

I lifted the top paper and began to read. "Emma is a pleasure to have in class. She always tries her best and never misbehaves. Outstanding in all subjects."

Agnes wrinkled her brow. "So you were boring even as a child?"

"I wasn't boring," I objected. "It says right here I was a pleasure." I tapped the paper.

"For a teacher, it may be a pleasure. In life, it's a guaranteed snoozefest." She pretended to yawn. "I'll admit, though, you get more interesting every day, especially since we discovered your true nature. Now you've got loads of potential."

I arched an eyebrow. "Potential for what?"

Agnes smiled. "Mischief and mayhem, of course."

"I should've known. Your two favorite vices," I said. I paged through the report cards. "Well, these aren't the letters, but it's fun to have a memento from my childhood. I can imagine the endless fun Gareth will have ripping apart my elementary school report cards."

"I'm glad today wasn't a complete waste of time," Agnes said. "Speaking of a waste of time, I need to move on to tiddlywinks. Let's vamoose."

For an elderly witch, Agnes moved like a rocket. I chased after her out of the activities room. She was halfway down the hall when a flash of color in the adjacent corridor caught my eye. I came to a screeching halt, nearly tripping over my own feet.

A body was sprawled across the floor.

"Agnes," I called. "I think someone's hurt. We need to call a healer." I hurried down the length of the corridor to reach the injured party. It was hard to tell from his crumpled position on the floor, but, based on the little horns and tail, he appeared to be a satyr.

"Sir, can you hear me? Can you tell me what's wrong?"

I checked for a pulse but felt nothing. Tiny droplets of green liquid were splattered on the floor beside him. He was on his stomach and looked like he might have been crawling for help.

"What is it?" Agnes said, appearing behind me.

I turned to face her. "I'm really sorry, Agnes, but I think this satyr is dead."

She paused a moment. "Dead, you say? Must be a Tuesday. Someone always seems to die on a Tuesday in the care home."

"Do you recognize him?"

"That's Titus," she replied. "He's a crotchety old fool. His room is at the end of the hall there."

So it *was* possible that he'd crawled from his room to get help. I wondered why no one had answered his call button. Maybe he hadn't used it.

"Any idea what this green liquid is?" I asked.

Agnes bent over to study the droplets. "Looks like the morning health drink. It's supposed to be chock-full of super vegetables and fruit, which is exactly why I avoid it. I'm too old to worry about good habits now."

A fairy nurse rounded the corner, a concerned expression on her face. "Is everything okay here?"

Agnes shrugged. "Well, the good news is that somebody is about to get bumped off the care home wait list. The bad news is somebody needs to inform Titus's family that he's dead."

"Thank you for your astute assessment, Agnes," the fairy said. "I need to get the medical team here immediately." She fluttered into the nearest room and I could hear her calling for help. I stayed on the floor next to Titus, unwilling to leave his side. It seemed a horrible way to die, on the dirty floor of the Spellbound Care Home.

"Don't look so upset," Agnes said. "Titus lived a full life. I hope you don't blubber like that when I pop off." She clucked her tongue.

"Agnes, don't say things like that," I said hotly. As annoying as Agnes could be, I preferred her alive. She was like a member of the family to me—a member of the family I avoided at holidays by reading in my room.

The healing team came rushing down the corridor with a stretcher and some kind of magical crash cart.

"Move aside, please," a pixie said.

I flattened myself against the wall, watching them work, but I knew it was to no avail. Titus wasn't going to walk these halls ever again.

I glanced at Agnes, who'd joined me against the wall. "What happened to tiddlywinks?"

"This seems more interesting," she said.

"Since when?" I queried. "You acted like a dead body was no big deal."

"It isn't to me," she replied. "But it clearly is to you."

My expression softened. "Agnes, are you showing compassion for me?"

She scowled. "Absolutely not. I just want to be first in line with the gossip come dinnertime. I bet I get an extra pudding out of it."

I grimaced. "Okay, Agnes. Whatever you say."

"Emma? What are you doing here?" Sheriff Astrid appeared in the corridor with her equally blond sister, Deputy Britta.

"She found him," Agnes replied, jabbing her thumb in my direction. "She sniffs out trouble like nobody's business. Must be her sorceress gene."

I glared at the old witch. "You said yourself that Titus lived a full life. There's no trouble."

"Then how do you explain the presence of the Valkyrie sisters?" Agnes asked.

"When a body is found in an unusual place, we need to check things out," Astrid said. "It's standard protocol."

"So if he'd been discovered dead in his bed, you wouldn't be here?" I asked.

"Not unless there were suspicious circumstances," Astrid replied.

"Cool," Britta said, peering at the floor. "Green stuff."

At the sight of the droplets, Astrid went into full sheriff mode. "Everybody step away from Titus."

The medical team stopped what they were doing.

"Are you sure?" a fairy asked.

"Unless you're about to tell me that he's still alive, then yes, I'm sure," Astrid replied.

"Yes, Sheriff," the fairy replied and fluttered out of the way, followed by the rest of the medical team.

"Britta, section off this area," Astrid ordered.

"Ooh, I can help with that," Agnes said. "I can do a protection spell."

I elbowed Agnes in the ribs. She wasn't supposed to be doing any magic in the care home. Our skills practice in the activities room was completely confidential.

"She means I can do one," I said.

"No, you can't," Agnes shot back, rubbing her stomach. "Not unless I help you."

Astrid smiled. "Thanks, but we can use good, old-fashioned tape. No magic required."

Agnes blew a raspberry. "Bo-ring."

"But effective," Britta said, and unrolled the tape around the area. She made sure that the onlookers were on the other side of the tape.

"Did anyone see him crawl out here?" Astrid asked.

"No. This is where I found him when I left the activities room," I said.

"You didn't hear anything?" Astrid queried,

I shook my head.

"Britta, poke your head in the rooms between Titus's and here," Astrid instructed. "See if anyone saw or heard anything."

"This is getting procedural," Agnes complained. "I'm heading to tiddlywinks."

"See you next time," I said. "Thanks for the help."

She waved without looking back and disappeared down the stretch of corridor.

"You two have the strangest relationship," Astrid remarked, while studying the satyr's body.

"It's not *that* strange," I said. "I think she's lonely."

"But Lady Weatherby's been visiting her more often, hasn't she?" Astrid asked.

"Off and on," I said. I didn't want to mention our private magic lessons in the care home. No one would support the idea of Agnes being around magic, not with her insane reputation.

A familiar figure floated down the hall. "Hey, Silas," I greeted the elderly genie.

"If it isn't the most beautiful sorceress this side of Curse Cliff," he said. His brow wrinkled as he noticed the heap on the floor. "Is that Titus?"

"I'm afraid so," I said.

Silas snorted with displeasure. "I mean, he wasn't anyone's shot of Goddess Bounty, but still. Tough to see him like this."

"Titus was difficult?" I queried.

"He made Agnes look like a Southern belle."

Astrid's ears perked up. "In what way?"

Silas drifted closer to the body but stopped short of the tape. "He was an ornery satyr. Bossed around the staff. Kept to himself, except when he felt like ruining game night. No visitors to speak of."

"None at all?" I asked.

Silas shook his head. "Even the healers' team argued over which one was assigned to him. Just last week, I overheard them arguing in the staffroom."

I squinted. "And what were you doing in the staffroom, Silas?"

He cleared his throat. "I wasn't *in* the staffroom. I was on the other side of the door."

"Doing what?" I could tell by his expression that he'd been up to no good. Typical Silas.

"That's irrelevant," he said.

"Why didn't they want to be assigned to him?" Astrid asked, as she combed the area for evidence. I watched as she opened a kit to swipe samples of the green droplets.

"Because he was a pain," Silas said. He glanced down at the satyr. "Sorry, friend, but you were. He barked orders at everyone and made the job intolerable for many here."

"Couldn't they boot him out of the care home?" I asked.

"Agnes said there's a wait list to get in. You'd think the care home would just refuse to put up with his nonsense."

"There's all sorts of bureaucratic red tape that prevents eviction," Silas said. "Usually it's a good thing to protect the rights of the elderly."

"But not in this case," I said.

"No, certainly not. Yet I still feel the desire to mourn him. Must be the sense of my own mortality." Silas gazed at the dead satyr, empathy stirring in his dark eyes. "Rest easy, old friend."

CHAPTER 4

I OPENED the front door and trudged inside, my mood dampened by the death of the old satyr. It didn't matter that he was a stranger. Because I was the one who discovered him, I felt a sense of responsibility.

The moment I entered the kitchen, I found myself awash in a wave of hostility.

"Daniel, what are you doing here?"

He turned to me and grinned. I immediately noticed the white apron tied around his waist that read *Guardian Angels Do It in the Kitchen*.

"What does it look like I'm doing?" he asked. "I'm making you dinner."

"He's making a mess in *my* kitchen is what he's doing," Gareth grumbled. "You should see the way he splashes grease everywhere. It's a culinary crime."

I ignored Gareth and focused on my angel's wings. The large white wings were splattered with some kind of sauce.

"What are you cooking?" I asked, sniffing the air for clues.

"One of my own creations," he said proudly. "Ale-battered meatloaf."

28

Gareth made a gagging noise.

"That sounds…interesting," I said.

Daniel squinted at me. "Interesting is bad. You'll love it. I promise." He planted a kiss on my forehead. "Now you go in the other room and sit down and relax. I know you've been working really hard."

I shot a quizzical look at Gareth, who only shrugged.

"Okay, I'll do that."

"Wait," he said quickly. "I have wine." He plucked a piece of stemware from the adjacent counter and handed it me. "From the local winery, of course."

"Naturally." I smiled and sailed out of the kitchen with my glass of wine and Gareth hot on my heels. As soon as we were out of earshot, I looked at my vampire ghost roommate. "What's going on?"

"He hasn't said," Gareth replied. "But you should see the dining room."

I stepped through the doorway and sucked in a breath. The dining room table was adorned with a row of vases, each one exploding with a riot of colorful flowers. The scent was overpowering and I began to cough.

"It's moments like these I'm glad I've lost the power of smell," Gareth said.

Magpie ran between us and jumped onto the table to investigate the interlopers. He stopped and sniffed each bouquet until he reached the end of the table.

"It's not your birthday, is it?" Gareth asked.

"No, not that I have any real sense of time here," I said. Not the way I did in the human world. I knew the days of the week, of course, but had lost all sense of months and seasons. Spellbound had its own magical weather system.

Daniel came up behind me and kissed my shoulder before setting a platter on the table. "First course is up."

"First course?" I queried. "How many are there?"

"Three," he replied. "But the third one is dessert."

"Um, I don't mean to sound ungrateful," I said, "but what's the point of all this?"

He spun around and regarded me. "The point? The point is that I love you and want to do something nice for you." He flapped his wings, punctuating his response, and hurried back to the kitchen.

"By the devil," Gareth complained. "What if he wants to move in? I told you he'd want to."

"He doesn't want to move in," I insisted. "He has a lovely house of his own."

Gareth folded his arms. "And what are you saying? That my house isn't lovely enough for an angel? A *fallen* angel, might I remind you."

"Gareth, you know I love this house," I said. With its beautiful stained glass windows and wraparound front porch, the rambling Victorian was my idea of a perfect home.

"What's Gareth moaning about now?" Daniel asked. "Is he jealous because he can't eat any of my delicious meatloaf?"

"Meatloaf is for dilettantes." Gareth's fangs popped out and I moved to stand between them. Even though Gareth was a ghost, I had no doubt he could do damage to Daniel if he really put his mind to it.

"Gareth, if you give Daniel and me some privacy, I'm happy to share this wonderful dinner with Magpie."

"Fine," Gareth huffed and disappeared. I knew he'd behave for the sake of his cat.

Magpie leapt onto a chair and looked at me expectantly.

"Not at the table," I said. "I'll put yours in the kitchen."

Magpie hissed before scampering off to the kitchen to await his prize.

Daniel and I sat at the table to enjoy our first course in peace and quiet. I smiled when I realized what the first course was.

"Roasted beets and goat cheese salad," I said. "I was expecting something more Spellbound."

He grinned. "You told me it was something you missed from the human world, so I thought you might like it."

I speared a few pieces into my mouth. "Like it? I love it. Thank you."

He took a long drink from his wine glass. "You seem a little down. Is everything okay?"

I told him about Titus, but not about the page with runes from the old grimoire. I wanted to wait until I had more information before I shared that with him.

"There's nothing you could've done to save Titus," Daniel said. "It sounds like he was already dead by the time you found him."

"He was, but I still feel bad. I wish I'd let Agnes go to tiddlywinks sooner. Then maybe we would've been in the hallway at the right time."

"You and I both know there are no time machines," he said.

"No, just dreams that allow us to time travel." I sipped the wine. It tasted delicious with the salad.

"But no do-overs," Daniel said.

"Sadly not."

"If you could go back in time and change one thing, what would it be?" he asked.

"Taking into account the butterfly effect or no?"

"No. Too complicated." He wiped his mouth with a napkin. "You think about it while I get the main course." He took away the salad plates and promptly returned with the meatloaf and a side of asparagus.

"This looks amazing," I said. I was hungrier than I realized. The salad had been enough to take the edge off, but now that I had a meatloaf in front of me, I wanted to devour it whole.

"So what's the verdict?" he prompted.

"Mine is easy," I said. "I would go back to the day my mother died and prevent her from drowning." That, in turn, would likely prevent my father's death. He'd been a changed man after she died. A shadow of his former self. Saving her would save him as well.

He placed a slice of meatloaf on my plate. "You wouldn't go back further and prevent your biological mother from giving you up?"

"No," I said. "I'd need to know more about her reasons before I made that decision."

"That's reasonable."

"What about you?" I asked. The meatloaf practically melted in my mouth. It was insanely good and I wasn't even a fan of meatloaf.

"I would go back to the point in time where I still had my halo and tell that angel not to be a fool."

I reached over and covered his hand with mine. "Look at it this way. If you still had your halo, we may never have met."

"Same goes for your mother," he said. "Although I have a feeling we would've met some other way. Sometimes it feels like we've always known each other."

"It does, doesn't it?" I chewed my food thoughtfully. "I think that's why I fell in love with you so quickly. It was like I recognized you on a deeper level."

He squeezed my hand and released it. "Same here."

"If you start kissing at the table, I'm moving out," Gareth complained.

I whipped around to see him hovering in the doorway. "What about our deal?"

"I was only coming through to check on Magpie. He's hungry, too, you know."

"Fine." I cut a few pieces of meatloaf into smaller chunks.

"I'll be right back, Daniel. Do you want me to bring in the dessert?"

"No, I'll do it," he replied. "I want to wait on you tonight."

"I feel like he broke your favorite vase or something," Gareth said.

I walked past him with Magpie's dinner. "He's being a thoughtful boyfriend. I think it's nice."

Gareth followed me to the kitchen. "Use the other bowl. The ale in the meatloaf will stain that one."

I rolled my eyes as I swapped out Magpie's bowls. The cat lunged for the food with a ferocity normally reserved for lions attacking gazelles. I averted my gaze and hurried back to the dining room. Thankfully, Gareth stayed behind in the kitchen.

"So is there another reason you're being so thoughtful tonight?" I asked. "Other than your usual good nature?"

Daniel hesitated. "There is something I'd like to talk to you about, but it can wait until dessert."

"Nothing bad, I hope."

"No, of course not. Don't worry."

I scarfed down the rest of the meatloaf and asparagus with superhuman speed and waited for the delivery of dessert.

"Burstberry pie," I said, delighted.

"For this one I cheated," Daniel said. "I bought it at the bakery, but only because I ran out of time."

"It's the thought that counts," I said, shoveling an over-sized bite into my mouth. My grandmother would be appalled by my manners right now.

"I've been wanting to talk to you about our relationship," Daniel said.

"Didn't we just do that?" I asked. "And we both agreed it's great?"

He chuckled. "Yes, but I'd like to say more, if that's okay. I

33

feel like it's something we've been dancing around for a while. We have the emotional connection that was missing from all my other relationships."

Heat burned the back of my neck and my cheeks. "And you're wondering why we don't have the physical connection..."

"No, not at all." He frowned. "In fact, I think the physical connection is every bit as strong as the emotional one."

"But we haven't *fully* connected," I said. "Physically, I mean."

He gave me a mischievous grin. "Not yet, but there's plenty of time for that."

"You don't mind waiting, do you?" Egads, I hated to even ask.

"For you? I'd wait an eternity."

Relief swept over me. "That's sweet," I said. "But an eternity is probably overkill."

He leaned back against the chair. "I'm not saying it's my preference. I'm just letting you know that I'm all in, no matter what the pace is."

"I'm glad to hear it," I said. I truly was. Not that I doubted Daniel's devotion for a second, but it was always nice to have reassurance.

"You are, without a doubt, the love of my extended life, Emma Hart. There's no one in the world I'd rather wait for than you."

It took every ounce of self-restraint not to jump him right then and there. Patience was a virtue, but even I had my limits.

The bone cottage looked the same as the last time I'd visited Raisa. I wasn't sure how I expected it to be any different since the owner was dead. Raisa wasn't going to be heading down to the garden center for perennials anytime soon.

A gust of cold air blew through me and I shivered. Despite my good relationship with the departed witch, her house never ceased to scare the daylights out of me. To be fair, skulls and bones as decoration was likely to make anyone ill at ease.

Do we have to come here again? Sedgwick complained, flying overheard and slightly to the left, as requested.

"You don't, but I do," I called. "Go home if you're a scaredy cat."

How dare you insult me, he replied. *The proper term is scaredy owl.*

"Don't worry. Raisa won't bite you," I said. If she did, those iron teeth would cut through an owl's feathers like a chef's knife. I shuddered.

Why did you shudder? Sedgwick asked.

"Because the air is cold," I lied.

You do remember I can read your thoughts.

Minotaur shit.

Standards, Your Highness.

I strode to the front door and knocked politely, ignoring the empty eye sockets of the skull above my head. The door creaked open and I stepped inside.

"Are you coming in?" I called to Sedgwick.

I'll wait out here, he replied, sounding displeased.

"I'm sure you can find a few mice in the forest," I said, and closed the door behind me.

"He surely can," Raisa said. "Welcome back, my pet."

"Good to see you, Raisa." I faced the ghostly witch. Well, she wasn't ghostly like Gareth. Her form was solid, whereas my vampire roommate had a more ethereal quality.

"Can I offer you a spot of tea?" she asked. "Two fingers of whiskey, perhaps?"

"No, thank you." Not unless I could be convinced there weren't actual fingers involved.

Raisa clicked her iron teeth. "What brings you back to see a lonely old witch?"

"I need your help," I said, and retrieved the parchment from my cloak pocket.

Her eyes lit up. "Ah, what is this?"

I spread the parchment flat on a nearby wooden table. "A copy of a page. Laurel found the original in the coven library pressed inside an old grimoire. The writing had been hidden by a concealment spell."

"How fascinating." Her eyes traveled over the paper and she made an occasional excited sound.

"Can you read it?"

"They're runes. Of course I can," she said. "I'm dead. I can read anything. If you happen to find anything in Scottish Gaelic let me know. It's a personal favorite."

If it were true that the dead could read any language, then I could've asked Gareth for help. I wasn't convinced Raisa was right about the skills that accompanied death.

"Laurel is working on interpreting the runes, but I thought you might be able to help us."

She eyed me curiously. "You came to me and not Lady Weatherby?"

"The coven tends to tie things up in rules and regulations. We didn't want that."

"A wise move, my pet." Raisa's bony finger trailed along the thick, yellowed paper and her lips moved, though no sound came out. As much as I wanted to be patient, I found myself shifting my weight from one foot to the other. I stopped just short of tapping my foot.

"Stop distracting me, sorceress," she scolded. "You're like a jumping pepperschnitzel."

"I don't know what that is."

"Doesn't matter. Just stop acting like one."

I tried to remain perfectly still. "Well?"

"Don't rush a dead witch. It's bad manners."

"I'm sorry. I'm excited," I said.

"Go home and kiss your heavenly boyfriend if you're excited. I'm trying to read." She popped out an eyeball and held it in her hand.

"Wouldn't two eyes work better?" I queried.

"This one is blurry." Raisa waved around the eyeball in her hand. "Do you and your friends have any idea what you've discovered?"

"Something that someone wanted to keep hidden."

She pushed her eyeball back into its socket. "My dearest sorceress, it's a way out."

I balked. "A way out? Of Spellbound?"

Raisa nodded. "The first step toward freedom."

I could hardly believe my ears. "How?"

"Whoever is responsible for writing this..." She tapped the runes. "They were piecing together a way to reverse the curse on the town from other sources. The first step is this top section here."

I squinted at the stick-like characters. "Why would they hide it? Isn't that what everyone wants? To break the curse?"

Raisa lifted her bony shoulders. "Perhaps they hoped to be sure of its efficacy first. Who knows?"

"There's no way to tell who did it?" I asked. If the paranormal was still alive, why had they stopped working on it? And if the paranormal was dead, why not share the information beforehand?

"No way to tell from this." She peered at me. "It's a summoning. The first part."

"What's a summoning?"

Raisa rolled her eyes and I worried one would pop out again. "What is that Weatherby fool teaching you at the ASS

Academy? A summoning is a special spell where you call upon a being to appear."

"What kind of being? An enchantress?"

"In this case—a sacred unicorn." Her eyes grew brighter and more alive than usual, inasmuch as that was possible for a ghost with removable eyeballs.

My heart began to race. "I want to know as many details as you can interpret. Does it give us the actual spell for someone to perform the summoning?"

"Not just *someone*, my pet" Raisa corrected me. "But someone pure of heart and mind. You can't expect a sacred unicorn to interact with just anyone."

My gaze met hers and I knew what she was thinking. She'd fed me a potion when we'd first met. It was called the Pure of Heart test. Thankfully, I'd passed or the potion would have killed me.

"You think *I* need to summon the unicorn?" I queried.

She shrugged her thin shoulders. "We could serve out the Pure of Heart potion to others and see which ones drop dead and which ones survive."

That didn't seem like our best option. "Is that all it says?"

"No. The purpose of summoning the unicorn is so you can remove its horn," she said. "The horn is necessary for the next step in breaking the curse."

My hand flew to my chest. This was an unbelievable find. Laurel would be so proud of herself when she found out. This was the type of discovery that deserved statues or buildings named after her. Maybe Arabella St. Simon would need to step aside for Laurel.

"This information is hopeful, but not certain," Raisa warned. She must have sensed my enthusiasm. "You must tame the unicorn in order to remove its horn. You cannot take it by force. It must be mutually agreed upon."

"So I ask it nicely?"

Raisa cackled. "If only life were that simple. You are missing an important question."

"What's that?"

"How do you tame the unicorn?"

"Besides being pure of heart and mind?" I glanced at the parchment. "Does it tell us?"

"There's a certain ancient requirement for taming a unicorn," she replied. "It doesn't need to be written. Everybody knows."

When I looked at her blankly, she burst into a loud sigh.

"In order to tame a unicorn, you must also be pure of body. A virgin," she proclaimed, throwing her thin arms wide.

I balked. "Are you serious? A virgin? That's completely...sexist."

"Rules are rules. Purity is required," she said, unconcerned. "Pure of heart, mind, and body."

"Puritanical more like," I said hotly.

She examined me closely. "Whether you agree with it or not, the question is—do you qualify?"

I crossed my arms over my chest. "You're dead. I think you already know the answer."

She sniffed hard. "Life is wasted on the living."

"What's the rush?" I asked. "Neither of us is going anywhere." Unless we broke the curse... "So the runes also give us instructions on how to perform the summoning?"

"They do. I suggest you provide them to the coven for assistance."

I didn't look forward to that. We'd need to explain to Lady Weatherby how we came to possess the parchment in the first place. Hopefully she'd be so excited by the prospect of breaking the curse that she'd forgive Laurel's transgression.

"You should know, pet, that it will not be a matter of

walking up to the magical beast and proclaiming your purity."

"Oh no?" I queried. "Should I have my v-card ready to present as official documentation?"

Raisa moved around and scooped up a frog that had escaped from one of her mason jars. She shoved it back inside and sealed the lid. "There will likely be certain obstacles to overcome."

Obstacles. Terrific. Because being trapped in a paranormal town wasn't enough of an obstacle.

"What kind of obstacles?" I asked.

Raisa smiled. "That's the beauty of magic. The obstacles will manifest when the chosen participant is ready to begin."

"Within the borders of Spellbound?" I asked.

"Where else?"

"But how? In the woods? In the hills?" I pictured the bounce house obstacle course that Markos owned. Somehow I doubted it would be that simple.

"The details I have no knowledge of," she replied.

"Will I have to swim?" I asked. My palms began to sweat just thinking about it. Would I suffer the same fate as my mother? Was the universe really that cruel? What if one of the obstacles involved heights? I was awful with heights. I'd have to remember to take a double dose of my anti-anxiety potion before I started the summoning.

"Try to relax," she said. "You don't want to suffer a heart attack before you even begin. I only know that you shouldn't expect a—what is the human expression—a walk in the park. Nothing worth anything is easy. I'm sorry. I wish I could offer more."

"Don't be silly, Raisa," I said. "You've cracked the code. You've been an enormous help." I glanced at the runes on the page. "What about the rest of it?"

"Let's not worry ourselves with that now," she said. "If

you cannot acquire the horn, then the rest is of no consequence."

No pressure then.

The dead witch's eyes blazed with hope. "And to think this might lead to the end of the curse. Incredible."

"That's the idea," I said, folding the copy of the parchment. "We need that unicorn horn." I paused. "But, Raisa, since you're dead, does breaking the curse really matter to you?"

"While it's true I won't be free to leave, pet, at least it means that others will be." Her expression softened. "I should like that. Plus, new blood in town. Could be fun for me, right? A few new unsuspecting paranormals to petrify."

I suppressed a smile. "Raisa, you're terrible."

She flashed her iron teeth. "But you love me anyway."

I sighed and slid the paper back into my pocket. "So help me, I do."

CHAPTER 5

I STARED at the dying plant on my windowsill and sighed. "Althea," I called.

My Gorgon assistant appeared in the doorway between our offices, her headscarf firmly in place.

"You rang, my liege?"

"Hardy har," I said. "Keep it up and I'll start calling you Sedgwick."

Althea gave me a pointed look. "Do that and see how my snakes respond."

I blinked my eyes innocently. "I'm no nature expert, but don't owls eat snakes?"

She opened her mouth for a snarky reply, but then snapped it closed again. It was fun to get the upper hand with a Gorgon sister on occasion. It happened far too rarely.

"Why is that plant dying?" I asked, gesturing to the windowsill. "You always make such a big deal about how you take good care of them."

Althea sashayed over to the window to investigate. "This is bizarre. I've been taking excellent care of Mr. Greensleeves."

"You named a plant Mr. Greensleeves?"

She whirled around to look at me. "You have car named Sigmund and a wand named Tiffany. Need I go on?"

"Point taken," I mumbled.

Althea touched the wilting leaves. "Something isn't right." She sniffed the soil. "Let me take him into my office and see what I can do."

"Thanks," I said. "I know I'm not the best with keeping things alive, but you've been doing such a good job."

"I sure have," she said, and, that quickly, the sassy attitude was back. She sailed into her office and closed the door behind her.

An unexpected knock on the door jolted me. "Come in," I yelled.

Astrid's blond head appeared. "Hey there. You busy?"

I waved her in. "Just investigating the murder of my plant," I joked. "Maybe you can help Althea assess the evidence. How are you?"

"I got the autopsy results for Titus," she said, dropping into the chair in front of me. I could tell from her expression that the news wasn't good.

"Murder?"

She nodded solemnly. "Murder."

I whistled. "What does the report say?"

"Those green droplets weren't part of the meal plan. They were poison."

I winced. "Poor Titus." No matter how anyone felt about him, poison was a terrible way to die.

"We've identified it as a potion called Organ Massacre."

"Subtle," I said sarcastically. "I can't imagine what the potion does."

"I'm heading over to the care home to interview a few folks," Astrid said. "Do you want to come or do you have a case?"

"No case," I said, except the Case of the Ancient Parchment, which was still tightly under wraps until I spoke with Lady Weatherby. "Where's Britta?"

"She had an appointment with Boyd," Astrid said. "I told her not to cancel."

"Why the healer? Is she sick?"

"She's been suffering from headaches lately," Astrid said. "Could be eye strain, but I think it's connected to her bad dreams."

My brow creased. "I thought her sleep had improved since she started harp therapy."

"But then she had an argument with someone in the class and stopped going," Astrid said. "So the dreams came back."

"Ugh. I'm sorry. I didn't realize that." I'd been so preoccupied with other issues, I'd stopped showing up for harp therapy. I didn't know that Britta had stopped as well.

"I'm hoping there's a tonic or potion he can give her," Astrid said. "I hate to see her so miserable. She can barely function some days."

"Are you sure there's a physical cause?" I asked. "Sometimes depression can manifest as physical problems."

"Depression?" Astrid repeated. "Britta's not depressed. She's always been on the sullen side, but that's her cloudy personality."

"Okay," I replied. I could tell I wasn't going to get anywhere with this conversation right now. "I'm happy to come with you to the care home." It was always a good idea to catch Agnes off-guard and make sure she was behaving herself.

"Great." She slapped her palms on the arms of the chair. "Can we stop at Brew-Ha-Ha on the way? I've been running myself ragged since early this morning and could use a shot of adrenaline."

"Brew-Ha-Ha? You never have to ask me twice." I walked

over to Althea's door and cracked it open. "I'm heading out with Astrid. If you need me, send an owl."

"Don't mind me," Althea called back. "I'm just trying to revive our beloved Mr. Greensleeves."

"Guilt doesn't suit you, Althea," I said, and closed the door. "Lead on, Sheriff."

As soon as we stepped inside the coffee shop, I spotted the back of Begonia's blond head at a table across the room. Demetrius was with her. I caught his eye and waved.

"So are they a thing now?" Astrid asked.

"So far," I said.

"I thought he had the hots for you," the Valkyrie said.

"He's not an idiot," I replied. "He could tell that my feelings for Daniel were rock solid. There was no point in waiting for me to change my mind. Besides, I don't think it was ever about me. I think he liked the idea of fresh blood in town." I winced at my choice of words.

Astrid stepped up to the counter to order, keeping a careful eye on the new couple. "Do you think he's genuine about Begonia, though? He doesn't have the most trustworthy reputation when it comes to women."

"I wouldn't be able to change her mind even if I wanted to," I said. "She's had a crush on him since before I came to Spellbound. Besides, I do think Dem has changed."

"Why? Because he was interested in you?"

"No, because if Daniel can change, anyone can," I replied.

Astrid ordered a latte with a shot of adrenaline for herself and I ordered a cappuccino with a splash of honeytongue for me.

"You don't usually get honeytongue," Astrid said.

"I know, but if we need to sweet-talk anyone in the care home, I figure I'll be in a good position to ask questions."

Astrid tapped her temple. "Always thinking, Hart. That's one of the reasons I like having you around."

We took our cups to go and swung by Begonia's table on the way out.

"You two look cozy," I said. "Coffee date?"

Begonia blushed. "I'm telling him about my new tattoo ideas for Spelled Ink. Demetrius suggested meeting now since he had to cancel our plans tonight."

My brow lifted. "Oh? Something suddenly came up?" It was a Brady Bunch television reference that I knew no one here would get.

"I need to help a friend with a project," Demetrius said. I was immediately suspicious of his evasive tone. Egads, maybe I'd spoken too soon. Maybe Dem hadn't changed after all.

"Well, at least you're able to spend time together now," I said diplomatically. "I'm sure Demetrius has good ideas for your business."

"I can hardly keep up with his ideas," Begonia said, gazing at Demetrius. She may as well have had red cartoon hearts pulsing in her eyes.

"Where are you two headed?" Demetrius asked. "Looks more official than poker."

"Unfortunately, it is," Astrid said. "We're investigating an incident at the care home."

Begonia gasped. "The dead satyr you told me about?"

Astrid jerked her head toward me. "You blabbed?"

I grimaced. "Sorry. I didn't realize his death was a secret."

"To be fair, the fact that he died isn't a secret," Astrid said. "Now that we know it's murder, though, the care home is going to want to keep this as quiet as possible."

I pretended to lock my mouth and throw away the key.

"We're going now to speak to the staff and get a list of visitors for that day. Talk to some of the residents," Astrid said. "Keep it to yourselves, though, until we have more information."

"Good luck," Demetrius said. "I don't envy you."

"Thanks," I said. "Have fun building an empire, you two."

Astrid and I skirted the perimeter of the coffee shop and made our way toward the exit. Once we were free and clear of vampire hearing, I inched closer to her.

"He has to help a friend with a project?" I queried. "That's the lamest excuse I've ever heard. I'm totally following him tonight."

Astrid bit back a smile. "I was thinking the same exact thing. Too bad I've got a dinner at the Mayor's Mansion or I'd go with you."

"That sounds so official. Lucy really seems to be settling into the role nicely," I said.

"She's great," Astrid agreed. "She handles the different factions really well. Mayor Knightsbridge always had a bit of a superiority complex, but Lucy doesn't suffer from that, thank the gods."

"No, she really doesn't."

We drove in Astrid's jalopy to the care home on the northeastern side of town.

"Will you tail Demetrius by yourself or bring a friend?" Astrid asked, her eyes fixed on the busy road. "Take it from me, spying on a vampire isn't easy. Their senses are far better than ours."

"Best to go alone, I think. I'll need to use cloaking magic," I said. Or I could turn myself invisible. That seemed like a risky option for the purpose of checking up on Demetrius, though.

"What about Daniel?" Astrid suggested. "Could he go with you?"

I snorted. "Daniel would flip his halo if he knew I

47

intended to follow Demetrius at night. I think he's still jealous of our relationship."

"But you don't have a relationship with Demetrius," Astrid pointed out. "You have one with the cloud hopper."

"True, but Daniel has an ego and he's not afraid to show it."

Astrid shook her head. "Men."

"I know, right?"

CHAPTER 6

WE ENTERED the lobby of the care home and approached the reception desk. Monique was busy checking in a visitor. The fairy was one of many in a revolving door of receptionists. She smiled at us once she'd let the elf through.

"Emma, you know you can't bring drinks in with you." Monique nodded toward our lattes.

"We'll drink them here before we go in," I replied.

Astrid's brow creased. "Why can't we bring lattes inside?"

I cleared my throat. "Some people, in the past, may have been known to sneak other kinds of drinks in to give to certain residents. Maybe even used a coffee cup to hide alcohol. I'm not naming any names."

Astrid pursed her lips. "You did that?"

"No names," I shot back.

"Are you both here for Agnes?" the fairy asked.

"Not today," I said. "The sheriff has a few questions about Titus."

The fairy's smile faded. "Yes, what a terrible day that was."

"I need a list of all the visitors from that terrible day,"

Astrid said. "As well as a list of all the staff he interacted with."

"I'll let the director know you're here," she said. The fairy disappeared and we made ourselves comfortable in the seating area.

"Anders, you get back here," a voice called. The door to the corridor flew open and a small troll tumbled out into the reception area.

A woman burst through the doorway after him. Anders doubled over with laughter.

"You should see your face, Mom," he said. "You're beet red."

"I'm glad you think that's funny," his mother replied. "Because you'll be laughing about it in your bedroom for the rest of the day."

The small troll's face fell. "You're punishing me?"

"Of course I am. You were warned not to run. Twice." She held up two pudgy fingers. "You don't get a third chance."

"I don't want to come here in the first place," Anders complained. "It smells funny."

"That's the stench of death," a familiar voice said. Agnes slithered out of the corridor and into the reception room.

"Agnes, what are you doing out here?" I demanded. "You'll get in trouble."

"I sensed a disturbance in the force," she said. "I figured it could only be you."

"Liar," I said. "You heard Monique tell someone we were here."

Agnes rolled her eyes. "Okay, fine. That's also how I knew it was safe to sneak out here." She motioned to the empty desk. "No one's on duty."

"Is that typical?" the troll asked, her expression nervous. "I've just left my father-in-law here and I was assured the facility is safe."

Astrid stood and introduced herself. "Not to worry, Mrs…"

"Vera Bridge," she replied.

"Duncan's your father-in-law?" Agnes queried.

She nodded and placed an arm around her son. "We moved him in today. My husband seems calm about it, probably because he was here recently for a tour and knows it's a good place." She shivered. "I'm still a bundle of nerves."

The door jerked open and two smaller trolls spilled into the reception room.

"You're supposed to be with your father," Vera said.

"He's behind us," one the boys said.

Sure enough, a larger troll appeared a moment later.

"David, they're supposed to be with you," Vera chastised him.

David fixed his sons with a hard stare. "You boys know better than to tear down the hall like that. There are older residents here. They can't move fast enough to get out of your way."

"Damn straight," Agnes said, giving the boys a sharp look. "And some of us aren't afraid to use magic in retaliation."

I cleared my throat. "What Agnes means to say is that she prefers the care home to be a place of calm reflection."

Agnes grunted. "Sure. That."

Vera shot her husband a disapproving look. "David, when I asked you to keep the boys close, I didn't mean it. I don't want to be responsible for everything."

He gesticulated wildly. "I tried. They move like pixies on adrenaline."

The fairy reappeared with Howell Sanders, the Director of Care, in tow.

"Sheriff, Emma," Howell said. "Good to see you both." He narrowed his eyes at Agnes. "And what, may I ask, are you doing out here?"

"She was making sure my boys found their way out," Vera interjected. "They were lost in the hallways and she guided them out."

For once, Agnes kept her mouth shut.

"I think my father's room is down the hall from yours," David told her. "His name is Duncan."

"If he's in Titus's old room, then he's in a different hall," Agnes said.

Inwardly, I groaned. Naturally, Agnes had no qualms about mentioning the dead satyr.

"We were sorry to hear about Titus," Vera said. "I host a monthly book club at the house and his daughter is a member." Vera shook her head. "So sad."

"Titus has a daughter?" I queried.

Vera nodded. "Sadie. A lovely nymph."

"We're required to notify next of kin when a resident dies," Howell explained. "It's standard operating procedure." His expression made it plain to us that Sadie was advised of the death only and not the suspicious circumstances. Astrid and I kept the reason for our visit to ourselves. No need for Duncan's family to know that the last man in their father's bed had been murdered.

"I'd be horrified if you didn't notify the family," David said.

Howell clapped the troll on the back. "Not to worry, Mr. Bridge. Your father is in excellent hands. Agnes, head back to your room, please. I have business to conduct with these fine ladies."

"Nice to meet you," I said to the Bridge family. "See you later, Agnes."

She stuck out her tongue as Howell ushered us through the door and down to his office. Very mature. He secured the door behind us and his expression shifted to panic mode. "It was murder, wasn't it?" He covered his face with his hands. "This is awful. We can't let word get out."

"I can try to keep it quiet," Astrid said, "but not to the extent that it jeopardizes my investigation."

"Of course," Howell said. "I completely understand." He handed a leather-bound book to Astrid. "Here's the log for visitors. I've marked the page for the relevant date. I've also asked one of the nurses to bring me a list of staff that attended to Titus that day."

"I understand he was an unpopular resident," Astrid said.

Howell hesitated. "He wasn't one of our more affable ones, that's true."

"What about his daughter, Sadie?" I asked. "Was she a regular visitor?"

"Not to my knowledge," Howell said. "Then again, there are far too many to keep track of. That's why we keep logs."

Astrid opened the book and I scanned the list of names over her shoulder.

"There weren't too many visitors that day," I said. "I guess that helps."

Astrid reviewed the names. "No one actually came to see Titus at all."

"I guess it shouldn't be a surprise," I said. "We still need to speak with anyone else who visited that day."

Astrid groaned. "Phoebe Minor?"

I snatched the paper from her. "To see someone here?"

"Someone called Silas," she replied.

I whistled. "He's a genie here. I bet Agnes didn't like that one bit. I'm surprised she didn't mention it during one of her countless tirades against humanity."

"I'll have a copy of the names written and get this back to you," Astrid said.

I held up a finger. "I know a spell that can help with that." It felt nice to have useful magic to offer.

Monique opened the door and fluttered in. "I have the staff list."

"Perfect," Howell said. "Please give it to the sheriff."

Astrid took the list and gave it a quick look. "Can I speak to these employees now?"

"If they're here," Howell said. "By all means. I'll set you up in here."

"If it's all the same to you, I'd prefer to walk around," Astrid said. "I tend to pick up more information that way."

Howell smiled. "You are quite an improvement over Sheriff Hugo, aren't you?"

"I like to think so," Astrid said.

We left the office and headed toward the nurses' station.

"Is Mara here?" Astrid asked.

"I'm Mara," a nymph said, raising her hand.

"Hi, Mara," I said, in an effort to put her at ease. "I'm Emma and this is Sheriff Astrid. We understand you assisted Titus on the morning of his death."

Mara's eyes grew round. "I served him breakfast. That's all."

"What did you serve?" Astrid asked.

Mara looked thoughtful. "I'm not sure. Whatever was on the menu. I don't do any special requests."

"Did Titus ever make special requests?" I asked.

"All the time," Mara said. "For a while, we catered to his whims, but he got ridiculous. Like he wanted to see how far he could get us to bend."

"Sadist," Astrid muttered.

"That's what Hem called him," Mara said. "That's why they ended up in a fight."

Astrid and I exchanged glances.

"Who's Hem?" I asked.

"Hemingway. One of the orderlies," Mara replied. "He didn't like the way Titus treated us. Last week, he heard Titus call me a..." She lowered her gaze. "A not-nice word. Hem came barging into the room and nearly punched Titus right in front of me."

"Where can we find Hem now?" Astrid asked.

Mara glanced at the clock. "Probably in the kitchen."

We found Hemingway standing in front of the trash bin. He was a tall goblin with tattoos of nymphs covering his muscular arms.

"Hemingway?" Astrid queried.

His expression darkened when he noticed us. "You're the new sheriff, right?" He glanced at me. "And you're the one who visits crazy Agnes."

"She's not crazy," I objected. "Just eccentric."

He barked a short laugh. "Sure. Whatever you say. That old witch is bonkers in my book. Sometimes I clean out fifty pudding containers from her room in one weekend. How can an old lady eat so much pudding?"

Inwardly, I cringed. I knew exactly what Agnes was doing with that pudding, and it was safe to say she wasn't eating it.

"We're not here to talk to you about excessive pudding use," Astrid said. "We'd like to talk about your interactions with Titus."

He grimaced. "Ugh. That satyr made everyone's life here a misery. Is that the kind of interaction you mean?"

"I understand you had words with him not long before he died," Astrid said.

"You took issue with a name he called Mara," I added.

Hemingway folded his arms and his muscles bulged even further. "Yeah. So what? Someone had to step in. That old satyr was disrespecting staff here left and right and Howell Sanders did nothing about it."

"So you decided to take matters into your own hands?" Astrid asked.

Hemingway held up his hands. "I didn't touch the old timer. I wanted to—believe me. But I also need this job."

"Do you know how Titus died?" Astrid asked.

"Someone said he got hit in the back of the head," Hemingway replied. "That he tried to escape but collapsed in the hallway. That's where a visitor found him."

"I was the visitor," I said. "And he wasn't hit on the back of the head." The rumor mill was inaccurate even in the care home.

"Then how'd he die?" Hemingway asked.

"Poison," Astrid said. "Someone fed him a potion in the morning."

"Whoever it was, it wasn't me. I don't have access to no potions." He cracked his knuckles. "Just out of curiosity, what kind of potion was it?"

"A lethal one," Astrid said. "Someone would have had to mix it at home. It's not something you can buy premade in the shop."

Which also made it easier for the killer to cover their tracks. If they bought ingredients in different stores instead of all in one place, it would be harder to piece together.

"Goblins are lucky to get tonics for headaches," Hemingway said. "Nobody trusts us."

It was true that goblins didn't have the best reputation in Spellbound. I felt terrible that Hemingway felt discriminated against because of the bias.

"You should talk to the new mayor," I said. "Lucy is a friend of everyone in Spellbound. If you're feeling like you're being treated unfairly, go to the Mayor's Mansion and make an appointment."

Hemingway laughed. "You think I should just stroll my goblin butt up the steps of the Mayor's Mansion and knock on the door?"

I kept my expression neutral, trying not to picture his

butt walking up the stairs. The image was too comical. "Absolutely. Tell her Emma Hart sent you."

"Listen, if you want to talk to someone who had a real beef with Titus, talk to Gene Sutcliffe."

"Who's that?" I asked.

"Another resident here. He and Titus had it out over a game recently. Titus called Gene a cheater in front of the whole games room. It was nasty." He shook his head. "Old dudes can be hard core when it comes to their games."

"Was there a physical altercation?" Astrid asked.

"Dunno. I just know those two circled each other like lions fighting over territory whenever I saw them."

"And where's Gene's room?" Astrid asked.

"Same wing as Titus," Hemingway replied. "You won't be able to talk to him now, though. He's sedated. I only know because I had to push the gurney."

"Why is he sedated?" I asked.

"Dumb fool shifted and got stuck in one of the pipes. We got him out, but the healer had to sedate him when he shifted back to human because it hurt like hell."

Ouch. "What kind of shifter is he?" I asked.

"Dude's a wereweasel so the cheating thing is entirely possible, but Titus can't get away with saying minotaur shit like that because no one likes him." He paused. "Liked him, I mean."

"Thank you for your time," Astrid said. "And I'll have a word with Howell Sanders about being a little more proactive when there's a clear issue with a resident or member of staff."

Hemingway flashed a genuine smile. "Thanks, Sheriff. I'd appreciate that."

CHAPTER 7

Since Gene was unavailable for questioning, Astrid agreed that I should speak to Phoebe alone to see what I could find out. She dropped me off in front of the harpies' house and I noticed one of the Minors on the widow's walk at the top. I waved, not certain which harpy it was. Her giant wings folded behind her, the last evidence of her harpy form before she returned to her human shape.

I walked up the steps to the front porch and banged on the huge brass knocker in the shape of a bird with breasts. They weren't subtle about their natures, those harpies.

Calliope greeted me at the door. "Emma, what a pleasant surprise. Come in. You're just in time for tea."

Anytime seemed 'just in time for tea' in the Minor house. I could show up at midnight and I bet a pot of tea and finger sandwiches would be ready and waiting. I wondered whether harpies had typical sleep patterns. Somehow I doubted it.

"Thank you." I crossed the threshold and was, as always, struck by the clutter. The interior of the house was knick-knacks galore. Decorative plates covered every square inch of the walls. The button-eyed dolls with their vacant expressions gave me the heebie-jeebies. In the human world, the Minors would be prime candidates to star in a television show about hoarders. With her acid tongue, Octavia would most certainly become a tabloid and an internet darling.

I followed Calliope into the sunroom where most of her family members were already seated. A pot of tea, cups, and plates with cookies were on the large round table in the center of the room.

"Grandmother, look who's here," Calliope said.

Octavia Minor pursed her pruned lips. "If it isn't our plucky neighbor. Who's dead now?"

I stood awkwardly in the middle of the room, unsure how to respond.

"Grandmother, that's impolite," Darcy scolded. She was the eldest of the granddaughters and a permanent fixture in the community. If you had a cause, rest assured that Darcy was on hand to raise money for it.

"How is that impolite?" Octavia asked. "It seems like every time she comes around, it's because somebody's dead."

My fingers clenched. The matriarch wasn't entirely wrong, but still...I didn't want a reputation as a harbinger of death.

"Is Phoebe here?" I asked. "She's the one I need to speak with."

"Oh, you two are chummy now, aren't you?" Octavia asked. "A few harp therapy sessions and you're joined at her artificial hip."

"Let it be, Mother." Phoebe's voice came from behind me. "You're just jealous I have a life outside this house."

"I'd love for you to have a life outside this house," Octavia said. "If you'd all find a mate and leave the nest, maybe I'd finally get to enjoy my personal space."

"No one is stopping you from enjoying your life, Mother," Marisol said with a deep sigh.

"Says you," Octavia said. "You're the worst offender. You had three daughters and brought them here to live. It was bad enough when it was only you and Phoebe."

"Grandmother, think about what you're saying," Freya, the youngest granddaughter, said. "If we all moved out tomorrow, you'd be horribly lonely."

Octavia's chin jutted out. "I'd manage."

"Who would pluck your chin hairs?" Marisol asked quietly.

"I have a mirror and a pair of tweezers," Octavia snapped. "I'm good."

Phoebe groaned. "Enough already. I'm on my way out to Shamrock Casino and I don't need your negative energy hitching a ride." She looked squarely at me. "What do you need, little witch?"

"Can we talk in private?" I asked.

"Oh," Octavia said loudly. "Now they're trading secrets like schoolgirls. Next thing you know, Phoebe will have joined the ASS Academy." She harrumphed. "Strikes me as appropriate."

"Keep it up, old woman, and I'll throw you an early funeral," Phoebe shot back. "You're long past due as it is."

Calliope poured a cup of tea and brought it to me on a saucer. "Cookie?"

I cast a sidelong glance at Phoebe. I really, really wanted that cookie.

Phoebe sniffed. "Go on then. Gobble it down and then we'll talk."

"Thanks." I graciously accepted the cookie and set it on the edge of my saucer, careful not to let it tip over the edge.

"How's your houseguest?" Marisol asked.

"Which one?" Freya said. "She has a few now."

"Gareth and Magpie aren't guests," I said. "It's their house as much as mine."

Darcy took a dainty sip of her tea. "I believe Mother is referring to Daniel."

"Oh. Well, he's not my houseguest either," I said. "Daniel has his own house."

"Are you engaged yet after all that nonsense with Elsa Knightsbridge?" Octavia asked. She slurped her tea and smacked her lips together. "It was entertaining to watch, but I'm glad it's over."

"Grandmother," Calliope said sternly. "Emma's heartache was hardly entertainment for us."

"Oh, please." Octavia waved a dismissive hand. "It was all we could talk about in this house for a week. Let's not pretend otherwise."

"Let's *do* pretend," Darcy said, mortified.

"Daniel and I are not engaged," I said. "We're enjoying each other's company right now." It took so long just to acknowledge that we felt more for each other than friendship. There was no reason to rush the relationship, although I had no doubt in my mind that I wanted to marry him.

"I'd marry him in a heartbeat," Marisol said.

"That's because he has a pulse," Phoebe said.

"Not true," Octavia interjected. "She'd marry Demetrius Hunt and he doesn't have a pulse."

"Good point," Marisol said. "He's dating your friend now, isn't he?"

Ah, the Spellbound rumor mill hard at work as usual. "He is."

"What is it with the witches in this town getting all the action?" Phoebe complained. "Do I need to start wearing a black pointy hat and carrying a mangy cat under my arm?"

"I don't know anyone who fits that description," I said. I polished off my cookie and took a long sip of tea. Calliope had added one teaspoon of sugar, just the way I liked it. Now that was a good hostess.

"Don't forget, this one's a sorceress now," Octavia said. "She's been upgraded."

"I'm not a computer program," I objected.

"What's a computer program?" the eldest harpy asked.

Oops. "Something in the human world," I said.

"Come on, slowpoke," Phoebe said testily. "Your tea is finished and I want to get to the casino. Walk out with me and you can ask whatever it is you're dying to know."

We turned to go.

"She's not dying," Octavia yelled after us. "Someone else is already dead. Mark my words. That's why she's here."

I closed my eyes and prayed for strength. "Thank you for your hospitality," I called over my shoulder.

Once Phoebe and I were safely outside, I asked her about her visit to the care home.

"Why do you want to know about my visit?" Phoebe asked. I heard the note of suspicion in her voice.

"Because it corresponds to an incident with a resident."

Phoebe glared at me. "Incident, my rock solid behind. This *is* about a dead resident. Mother was right." She moaned. "I *hate* when she's right."

"Okay, fine. She's right. You happened to be at the care home the day Titus was found dead."

"That guy? No wonder you're here to talk to me." Phoebe gave a pointed look. "Although he was found by *you*, I understand." She continued to walk down the pathway and I hurried to keep up. She moved fast for an old harpy.

"Yes, but that's irrelevant," I replied.

"Why? You were at the care home the day he died, too. Are you being questioned? Oh, that's right. You're like best buddies with the sheriff, so you get a free pass."

"Phoebe, you know I'm not capable of murdering anyone. Besides, I didn't even know Titus."

"It doesn't mean you can't murder someone just because you don't know them."

I ignored her remark. "So the sign-in book says you visited Silas. Is that true?"

Phoebe stared straight ahead, continuing to walk at a brisk pace. "And what if it is?"

"His room isn't far from Titus's," I said. "Did you happen to overhear anything or see anyone suspicious?"

"I'm glad you're asking me this outside," she said. "Mother would lose her wings if she knew I'd been to see Silas."

"Why? What's wrong with Silas?" Other than the obvious issue of missing a crucial part of his body. As a genie, he had a human top half and a tornado-like bottom half. I didn't want to imagine the obstacles in his sex life.

"He lives in the Spellbound Care Home," Phoebe said. "That's what's wrong with him. Mother would never approve. She wants me to meet someone so I can live with him. I'm certainly not moving into the care home."

"Not with their insane waiting list," I said.

"Not because of the list," Phoebe said. "Because I'm not moving into a facility when I have a perfectly nice house right here."

"I didn't realize you were involved with Silas," I said. "Where did you even meet him?"

"I've known Silas for years," she said. "Then recently I went to a bingo night at the care home with a friend and Silas was there. Let's say we got reacquainted…in the broom closet."

I covered my ears. "Okay, I don't need the details."

Phoebe smirked. "Don't ask questions you don't want to know the answers to."

I steered the conversation back to Titus. "So you didn't notice anything odd when you visited him?"

"I didn't even see Titus. Just that witch friend of yours giving me the stink eye in the hall."

"Agnes?" Of course it was Agnes. Who else?

"For a former head of the coven, she's not very intimidating," Phoebe sniffed.

I laughed. "You may be the only one in Spellbound who feels that way."

A jalopy pulled alongside us. "What are you doing, Phoebe? I thought I was picking you up at the house?"

"I needed to have a private conversation with this one," Phoebe said, sliding into the passenger seat.

I peered inside to see an unfamiliar dwarf. "Hi, I'm Emma."

"This is Pam," Phoebe said. "She's my lucky friend, so I always make sure to go with her to the casino."

"Everyone needs a lucky friend," I said. "Have a good time. Be sure to leave enough pots of gold for other players."

"Fat chance," Phoebe called out the window as the jalopy sputtered away.

I stared at the horizon, lost in thought. So Phoebe hadn't seen or heard anything unusual. She hadn't even seen the victim. I was partly relieved. The last thing I wanted was to drag Phoebe Minor down to the sheriff's office for questioning. At least it was one name I could cross off the short list. Although it didn't lead me to the murderer, it was better than nothing.

"I found him," Gareth announced, materializing in the foyer. He grimaced when he noticed Daniel beside me. "I thought he might be gone by the time I got back. Some wishes never come true."

I ignored his jab at Daniel. "Good job. Where is he?" We'd decided to kill two birds with one stone—I needed to locate Demetrius and Gareth needed to practice leaving the house. He was still experimenting with materializing in other places in town, so this presented a golden opportunity.

"East end of town. Walking toward Thistledown Road." His expression soured. "And not alone."

"I'm on it. Thanks, Gareth." I pulled the hood of my cloak over my head and started for the door. "I'll see you both later."

"Wait for me," Daniel said.

I spun around to see the tall frame of the angel right behind me. "What are you doing?"

"What do you think I'm doing? I'm coming with you," he replied.

"I'm shadowing Demetrius and I don't want him to see me," I said. "How on earth do you think I'm going to hide over six feet of blinding white angel? It's not like you can disguise yourself as a pigeon."

Daniel scowled. "If you think I'm letting you go out at night to stalk vampires, then you need more therapy sessions on your calendar."

My eyes popped. "And if you think you *let* me do anything, then maybe *you* should consider starting therapy sessions. I love you, Daniel, but I make my own decisions. Right now I've decided to find out what Demetrius is up to."

"So have I," Daniel said stubbornly.

"Yes, but the difference is I want to find out for the sake of Begonia, my dear friend. You want to find out because you want one more reason to dislike Demetrius." I folded my arms and glared at him. "My motive is for the good of someone I care about. Can you say the same for yours?"

Daniel backed off. "Fine, but for the record, I don't like

this. Skulking around at night in order to follow a vampire strikes me as a bad idea."

"It's not just any vampire," I argued. "It's Demetrius."

"Yes, and you have no idea what he's doing. What if he's mixed up in something dangerous?"

I wiggled my magical fingers at him. "Then I am perfectly capable of defending myself. There's magic in these hands, remember?"

A slow grin brightened his handsome face. "Oh yes, I do remember."

I gave him a playful push. "That's enough of your innuendos, pervert."

"How about I wait for you here? Then maybe you can show off those magical hands when you get back?"

I jumped up and gave him a quick kiss. "I'll see you tomorrow, Daniel." I needed a good night's sleep and Daniel waiting up for me guaranteed the opposite outcome.

I parked Sigmund a few blocks over from Thistledown Road and walked the rest of the way on foot so that my car was out of sight. Just as Gareth said, Demetrius stood out front of a red brick building with a willowy brunette. Her hair was long and stick straight and her cheekbones looked like they were sculpted by the gods. I knew I'd never seen her before. There was no way I would forget a woman that beautiful. They laughed about something he said before entering the building together. I noticed her hand briefly touch his arm on the way in.

I studied the front of the building, but there was no sign or indication of what it was. A secret vampire hangout like our remedial witch lair? Was his companion even a vampire?

I waited a couple of minutes before braving the cobblestone and moving to stand in front of the building. I leaned my forehead against the glass and tried to peer inside. The building appeared to be empty. Why were they meeting here? Was this their secret love nest? Maybe she was married so they couldn't meet at her house and Demetrius worried about Begonia running into her at his house. All sorts of possibilities raced through my mind—none of them good.

I stood outside the door, debating my next move. Did I charge in after them and demand answers? I regretted not using the invisibility potion. Then I could follow him without the fear of being seen. I would have needed the girls' help for that one, though, and I didn't want Begonia to know what I was up to. I didn't want to tell her anything until I had more facts.

"Good evening, Emma," Stan said. The town registrar was heading home from a night at the pub it seemed, based on the zigzag pattern of the elf's walk.

"Hey, Stan," I said. "Looks like you had a fun night."

"I did, indeed. A lovely dinner at the Mayor's Mansion. It was far more relaxed than the parties Mayor Knightsbridge used to throw."

"That's good to hear," I said. "Astrid said she went to a dinner there recently and it was a nice mixture of paranormals. Was your dinner just elves?"

"Goodness no," he said. A burp escaped his lips and he covered his mouth with an embarrassed laugh. "I think that's why I'm so tipsy tonight. Those naughty werewolves got me good and drunk. I never realized how much fun they could be."

I smiled. "They do like to have a good time."

Stan seemed to notice the building I was loitering in front of. "What are you doing hanging around here? This place has been empty for six months."

My brow lifted. "Really? Why?"

"The owners are a couple who've separated. They're arguing over ownership."

I thought about the attractive woman inside with Demetrius. Was she one half of that couple?

"I'm taking an evening stroll to clear my head," I said. "Walking through town always lifts my spirits, especially at night when the stars are out. I love the soft glow of the fey lanterns, too. It's all quite peaceful."

Stan gave me a pleasant smile. "You have made this place your own, haven't you? I knew you'd fit right in the moment I laid eyes on you in my office. Do you remember?"

"How could I forget? It was the craziest day of my life. You're one of the first residents I met in Spellbound." I laughed. "You have that picture of werewolves playing poker behind you in the office. The first time I saw it, it really freaked me out." Now, of course, I found it highly amusing.

I heard noises inside the empty building and worried that Demetrius would see me upon exiting. I looped my arm through Stan's and guided him away from the door. "How about I walk you home? You look like you could use a steady hand."

Before I could get a safe distance away, the door to the building opened and Demetrius emerged with his mystery woman. His eyes widened slightly when he noticed me.

"Emma. What are you doing over this way?"

"I'm escorting Stan home after too much fun at the Mayor's Mansion," I said quickly. I fervently hoped that Stan didn't contradict my statement.

"Wow. Fun and Mayor's Mansion in the same sentence," Demetrius mused. "There's an oxymoron."

"Who's your friend?" I nodded toward the willowy brunette. She was even more striking up close. My heart sank for Begonia. If Demetrius was up to his old tricks, Begonia didn't stand a chance.

"This is Marcie," he said. "She's an old friend."

No doubt. For a vampire like Demetrius, they were all old friends.

"It's nice to meet you, Marcie," I said. "I'm Emma Hart."

Marcie flashed a set of perfectly white teeth. "A pleasure to meet you, Emma. I've heard so much about you. I can't believe we haven't crossed paths yet."

I was just about to dig for more information, when Stan clutched his stomach. "Stan, you're looking a bit green around the gills."

He swayed to the side. "If you really intend to help me home, I think we better get a move on," he said.

Demetrius gave me an amused shrug. "Good luck, Emma. Have a good night."

"You, too," I said. But not *too* good. Although my Good Samaritan routine took priority tonight, I was determined to find out more about Marcie and her relationship with Demetrius.

Thankfully, I managed to get Stan all the way home before he puked in his rose bushes. He thanked me for my assistance and stumbled up the porch steps.

"So confused," he mumbled. "I thought Demetrius was dating your friend."

"He is," I said. "Begonia. She's the loveliest witch you'll ever meet."

Stan frowned. "Then what's he doing out with the succubus? A vampire and a succubus is always a dangerous combination. Too much need for feeding on both sides." He unlocked his door and practically tripped over the threshold.

"Stan do you need me to come in with you?" I asked. As much as I didn't want to, I wasn't about to leave the elf in dire straits.

"No, no," he said, shaking his head. "I'm having a tall glass of water with a painkiller and heading straight to bed. Not even going to change my clothes first."

I smiled. "Sounds like a plan, Stan. Have a good night."

He gave a wave and closed the door between us. I walked back into town toward Sigmund, not sure what to think. So Demetrius was out with a succubus. A gorgeous succubus. I wasn't ready to tell Begonia yet. I still had a little bit more digging to do. If there was one thing being the defense attorney in Spellbound had taught me, it was that things were not necessarily what they seemed.

CHAPTER 8

THE FIVE REMEDIAL witches stood in a row in Lady Weatherby's office. The head of the coven stood behind her desk with Chairman Meow seated in the chair. If she'd had her wand pointed, the scene would have resembled a firing squad.

"Witches, it has come to my attention that you have a certain parchment in your possession," Lady Weatherby said, staring down her long nose at us.

I tried not to flinch. How did she find out? Raisa certainly didn't snitch.

"Will anyone acknowledge my statement?" she asked.

No one replied.

"I see. Let's start with the specifics. First I would like to know how you acquired such an important document," she said.

I focused my attention on the portrait above her head of Arabella St. Simon, the academy's namesake. For whatever reason, the sight of Arabella always calmed me when confronted with the head of the coven's austere personality.

Millie stepped forward and my heart sank. She was going

to sing like a canary. I should have known she wouldn't stick with us.

"One of us found the parchment in an old grimoire in the coven library," she said.

I relaxed slightly. So she didn't tattle on Laurel. That was a step in the right direction.

"How interesting," Lady Weatherby said. "You do realize that, as remedial witches, you are not permitted in the coven library."

"We do realize," Millie said curtly. "Which is why we kept the discovery a secret."

Lady Weatherby clasped her hands behind her back. "So you decided to keep a secret that could change the fate of an entire town, rather than admit that you were somewhere you were not permitted to be."

Millie hesitated. "Not exactly...."

"I would like to see this parchment, please, so that I may ascertain its authenticity." Lady Weatherby crooked her finger. "This is no time for denials. Whichever one of you has it, I insist that you hand it over immediately."

We exchanged nervous glances before Laurel took a step forward, gathering the courage to speak.

"I have the parchment," she said, removing the rolled-up page from her cloak pocket. "I removed it from the grimoire since it clearly didn't belong there anyway. We've been working together to decipher it." She handed the piece of paper to Lady Weatherby.

"And have you managed it?" Lady Weatherby asked. Her attention was fixed on the parchment in her hands.

"Yes, I believe we have," Laurel said, her eyes sparkling with excitement.

"Is that so? Tell me then. What does it say?"

As if eager to hear the results, Chairman Meow strutted across the desk and fixed his gaze on Laurel. He no longer wore the little twisted antler headdress that matched the head of the coven's, but his regal air was undeniable.

Laurel hesitated. I knew she was nervous about sharing what we had learned. The implications were far-reaching. Then again, if the head of the coven asks you for information, you would be a fool to withhold it. No one expected Laurel to keep quiet.

"It talks about the need for the horn of a unicorn as an ingredient required for the spell to break the curse," Laurel said.

Lady Weatherby's lips stretched into a tight smile. "Well, that's not so difficult. I believe Mix-n-Match carries unicorn horns, or at least pieces of them."

Laurel shook her head. "I'm afraid it's not that simple. It's a special horn, one that can only be gotten after successfully summoning a *sacred* unicorn."

Lady Weatherby's eyes narrowed. "Explain further."

"I'll show you." Laurel moved to the corner of the desk and gestured for Lady Weatherby to set down the parchment. Then she retrieved a second piece of paper from her cloak. "This is the translation of the first part."

Lady Weatherby's brow lifted. "Your translation?"

"It's been a group effort," Laurel said. We all had the good sense to keep quiet about Raisa's involvement. The coven would object to the exiled witch's assistance, dead or not.

Lady Weatherby said nothing. She studied both parchments, her gaze flicking between the original and Laurel's version.

"This is an incredible find, Laurel," Lady Weatherby said. "Am I right to assume it was you who discovered its existence in the first place?"

"You can assume it," Laurel said, straightening her shoulders. "But I won't admit to anything."

"I see." Lady Weatherby rolled up both parchments and

placed them in her desk drawer. "I shall need to bring these before the coven and decide next steps."

"What about the council?" I asked.

"The council will be the next to know," Lady Weatherby said. "As it stands right now, this is an internal coven matter. The parchment was located on coven property and studied by witches. Once we've had an opportunity to examine it further, then I shall introduce the topic with the council and suggest a course of action."

Lady Weatherby was nothing if not pragmatic.

I raised my hand slowly. "I know the coven needs to review everything, but I should probably be the one to summon the unicorn and try to retrieve the horn."

Lady Weatherby pressed her thin lips together. "Of course you do. And why, pray tell, is that?"

Since I couldn't invoke Raisa's name, I had to be vague. "Because I...meet all the requirements," I said.

"Plus, she's a badass sorceress," Sophie added. "If that unicorn gives her any problems, then blam!"

"No one is 'blamming' a sacred unicorn," Lady Weatherby said. She lifted one dark eyebrow. "Now tell me, Miss Hart, to which requirements do you refer?"

"The one that summons the unicorn needs to demonstrate a degree of purity. Because I've already proven I'm pure of heart thanks to a certain dead witch's potion, I'm the logical choice," I said.

"Don't forget the pure of body part," Millie hissed.

My cheeks colored. "Thank you for the reminder, Millie, but I hadn't forgotten." I sucked in a breath. "And I can tame the unicorn in order to remove the horn because I'm..." I searched for a euphemism but finally decided a straight answer was best. "I'm a virgin."

"I see." The head of the coven dipped her head slightly,

causing her twisted antler headdress to tip to one side. "I shall take the matter under advisement, but it shall be a coven decision."

I cleared my throat. "Um, you said you were going to put the issue before the coven, and then the council. Does that mean everyone in town will know…about me?" Not that I was embarrassed…Okay, I was mortified. And I worried that Daniel would be equally mortified to learn that the whole town knew such an intimate detail about his girlfriend.

"I shall use my discretion," Lady Weatherby replied, and I sighed inwardly with relief. It was the best I could hope for.

"So are we in trouble?" Begonia asked, an expression of concern etched in her pretty features.

Lady Weatherby eyed her closely. "Do you think you ought to be?"

Begonia chewed her lip. "Maybe."

"I have an appropriate punishment for your deception," Lady Weatherby said. "Instead of class tomorrow, you may come to coven headquarters and give it a thorough cleaning from top to bottom."

"What about the fairy cleaning service?" Millie asked.

"Easy enough to cancel them," Lady Weatherby said. "Allow you ladies a chance to shine." She paused, a smile playing upon her lips. "And to make things shine."

Spell's bells. A joke from Lady Weatherby. Would wonders never cease?

Sophie gulped. "Can we use magic?"

Lady Weatherby gave a curt nod. "I'd expect nothing less."

In the afternoon, Astrid and I went to the address the care home had provided for Sadie, Titus's daughter. There was no jalopy in the driveway and no one answered the door. As we returned to the sheriff's jalopy, a neighbor appeared on the front lawn.

"You looking for Sadie?" he inquired.

"We are," Astrid said. "Any idea where we can find her now?"

"Cemetery," the neighbor replied. "She left about fifteen minutes ago. I let her take a snapdragon from my garden." He nodded toward the bright yellow flowers in front of his house. "Told her she couldn't go empty-handed."

"No, of course not," I said. "That was kind of you."

"Losing a parent is tough," the neighbor said. "And she'd already lost her mom. Even as an adult, knowing you're an orphan is hard to process."

His remark hit home for me. "Thank you for your help."

We drove to the southern edge of town where Astrid and I spotted a lone figure in the cemetery.

"Do you think it's her?" I asked.

Astrid opened the door to the jalopy. "Only one way to find out."

We walked across the cemetery grounds and I was momentarily distracted by the headstones. Paranormals truly lived long lives. It was a good thing, too, since space was limited in Spellbound for burials. On the other hand, not all paranormals chose to be buried. I'd already witnessed a Viking-style funeral pyre. It was like live streaming the cremation process.

"Excuse me. Are you Sadie?" Astrid queried.

The nymph turned away from the grave, noticing us for the first time. "Yes?"

"Hope you don't mind the intrusion," Astrid said. "Your neighbor told us where to find you."

Sadie pulled a face. "Not much gets past Mr. Bell."

"We were sorry to hear about your father," I said. "I spend a lot of time at the care home, and I know he'll be missed."

Sadie grunted. "That's kind of you to say, but there's no need to shovel minotaur shit in my direction. We weren't particularly close."

I gestured to the single yellow snapdragon in front of the headstone. "And yet you've come to pay your respects."

"He didn't want a funeral," Sadie said. "I figure I may as well have my own little ceremony here. He was still my father, despite our lack of a relationship."

"Had you been to visit him in the care home recently?" Astrid asked.

Sadie gave a harsh laugh. "Visit my father? Why would I do that when he never bothered to visit me all those years growing up. I owed him nothing."

I knew what Astrid was thinking. Even though Sadie hadn't been to visit her father, it was still possible she paid someone to give him the potion.

"When was the last time you saw your father?" I asked.

Sadie stared at the fresh grave. "It was on my birthday."

"And when was that?" Astrid asked.

"My birthday ten years ago," Sadie said. "It was before he went to live at the care home. My mother threw a party for me and he showed up, uninvited. At least he had the decency not to bring that elf with him."

Ten years later and Sadie was still clearly bitter about the incident.

"Which elf?" Astrid asked.

Sadie's eyes flashed with anger. "Deanna. The elf he left my mother for."

"When did your parents divorce?" I asked.

"They didn't," Sadie said. "They were never married. My father was a satyr. He didn't believe in marriage." Her jaw tightened. "It became abundantly clear why not."

"So when he left your mother for Deanna," I began, "what happened? Why did you stop seeing him?" I wondered whether the bitterness between her parents was the reason, as often happened in divorce cases.

"My father was obsessed with Deanna," Sadie said. "Whenever he was meant to visit me or have me stay with him, he always came up with an excuse why he couldn't. Deanna always needed him. I never understood how he could choose a grown elf over his only child." Bitter tears formed in her eyes. "It was one thing to stop loving my mother. I never understood why he stopped loving me."

"So what made you come here?" Astrid asked. "Why not just ignore his death?"

Sadie glanced at her father's grave. "I had unfinished business. Things I wanted to say that I didn't have the courage to say when he was alive. For years, I wanted to have it out with him, but I didn't do it for my mother's sake. After she died, I considered it again, but by then he was going into the care home. I didn't see the point anymore."

"Has it made you feel better?" I asked, gesturing toward the grave. "Has it given you closure?"

Sadie shrugged. "I'm not sure yet. It was my therapist's idea. She thought it was worth a try. I've been angry with him for so long, and unable to form healthy relationships because of what he did to me." She stopped talking and shook her head. "No, I am not a victim. I do not need his love in order to have self-worth."

"Which therapist do you see?" I asked.

"Thalia," she said. "I've been going to her for years. She's wonderful."

"I go to Dr. Hall," I said. "They're in the same building."

Sadie shot me a curious look. "Wow. I don't think I've ever met someone who actually goes to Dr. Hall. What's she like?"

I bristled. "She's wonderful, too." Although I knew she had

a certain reputation, I felt defensive about my favorite vampire therapist. Okay, so her methods were unusual and she had an odd need to one-up me with her own tragic stories, but I couldn't deny that she'd helped me with my emotional growth.

"Tell us about Deanna," Astrid said. "Was your father still in a relationship with her when he died?"

"I wondered about that when I'd heard he went into the care home," Sadie said. "Truthfully, I did my best to shut him out completely, and that included any news about him. If he wasn't with her, I don't want to know. It would feel like the ultimate slap in the face, to be abandoned for a relationship that didn't even last."

"Sadie, can you think of any reason why someone would want your father dead?" Astrid asked.

Sadie's brow creased. "Besides my mother and I? I don't know." It finally dawned on her that she was speaking to the sheriff. "Wait a minute. I thought my father died of natural causes."

"I'm afraid not," Astrid said. "Based on the autopsy reports, your father was murdered with a potion. We're trying to track down who may have had a reason to murder him."

Sadie's brown eyes widened. "Is that why you're here talking to me? Was this an interrogation?"

Astrid shook her blond head. "Just a conversation, Sadie. If you think of anyone, though, please let us know. Despite your history with your father, I have to imagine you'd want to see his killer brought to justice."

Sadie stood there, considering the statement. To my complete surprise, she turned and spit on his grave. "On the contrary. Let me know when you find out who it was so I can shake his hand."

Astrid and I exchanged shocked glances.

"We'll let you get back to your closure," I said, and we headed back toward the jalopy.

So much for years of therapy. Maybe Thalia wasn't so wonderful, after all.

CHAPTER 9

"If it isn't my favorite patient." Dr. Catherine Hall stood behind the bar, preparing our weekly cocktails. Two Arrogant Bitches.

"I don't think you're supposed to have favorites," I said.

"Why not? I'm not your mother."

I held up a finger. "Which is the perfect segue into this week's topic."

She placed a glass on the coffee table in front of me. "Don't you want to pepper me with questions about Lord Gilder first? You know you want to."

I raised an eyebrow. "Isn't this *my* therapy session?"

Catherine waved a dismissive hand. "Oh, please. Like you're not desperate for the details."

I leaned forward, unable to hide my interest. "Okay, fine. I do want to know. How's everything going with you two?"

Catherine and Lord Gilder had been neighbors many years ago and had developed a deep affection for each other, though it never moved beyond that phase. They'd become reacquainted recently and seemed to be attached at the hip, much to my delight. I was immensely fond of both vampires and wanted to see them happy.

Catherine swirled her cocktail before taking a long sip. Anything to extend the anticipation. My therapist excelled in torment. I shuddered to think what kind of vampire she'd have been if she'd succumbed to the dark side of her nature.

"Life couldn't be better now that Lord Gilder is a permanent fixture," she finally replied.

I'd never seen her so cheerful. It was a remarkable improvement over her usual sour attitude.

"I'm glad to hear it," I said. "You deserve a little sunshine in your life." Based on our many conversations, I knew her path to Spellbound hadn't been an easy one.

"It's like we're making up for lost time." She shivered with pleasure. "I'd forgotten how charming he could be. Knocks your socks off." She winked. "And the rest of your clothes as well."

My hands flew to cover my ears. "TMI. Thank you."

Catherine laughed. "Ha! You're such a prude, Emma."

"I am *not* a prude," I said, straightening. "As a matter of fact, I've been thinking a lot about this very topic recently."

She narrowed her eyes. "You've been discussing your prudishness?"

I sipped my drink. "No, my purity." I winced the second the word left my mouth. Spell's bells, I couldn't get into this with Dr. Hall, not without saying too much about the parchment. I had to wait for the coven and council to make its contents public knowledge.

Catherine's brow lifted. "And?"

I plucked an imaginary thread on the cushion. "We're still discussing it."

"What's the hold up? You love him, right?"

"With the passion of a million Harry Potter fans times ten."

"And he loves you."

I nodded.

"So what's the problem?" she asked. She drained her glass and set it on the coffee table. "Where did my coaster wander off to? I swear the patient before you pockets them on the way out. She's a complete klepto."

"I don't think you're supposed to say that," I said.

Catherine cocked her head. "Why not? I didn't tell you her name was Wendy." She laughed. "Oops. Now I have."

I shook my head. "I hope you're not this forthcoming about me when the next victim…I mean, patient comes in."

"Nope. I told you already. You're my favorite." She fished a coaster out of her handbag and placed it under her empty glass.

"You keep coasters in your handbag?" I queried.

"You never know when you're going to come up against a sweaty glass emergency." She pinned her gaze on me. "Now tell me more about your fear of sex."

"I don't have a fear of sex," I objected.

"He's a smokin' hot angel and you're reasonably attractive," she said. "Is this about Elsa?"

"No, definitely not," I said. "Elsa was beyond his control. I know that." Elsa Knightsbridge was a fairy and Daniel's former girlfriend who took revenge to a whole new level, subjecting him to a love potion without his knowledge. She would've married him, too, if I hadn't stopped the wedding and returned Daniel to his senses in time.

"Do you want to be married first?" Catherine asked. "Because I can understand that."

"You can?" For some reason, I expected more judgment from my therapist.

She blew a raspberry. "No, I don't get that at all, actually. Marriage is a human construct that spilled over into the paranormal world."

I buried my face in my hands and groaned. "I don't necessarily need to be married, but I would like some kind of commitment from Daniel." Yikes. I didn't even realize I felt that way until I said it out loud. The magic of therapy.

"Because you don't trust him?" she queried. "Because he has a reputation as a womanizing fallen angel and you don't want to fall victim to his charms only to be abandoned later?"

I folded my arms and glared at her. "I thought you liked Daniel."

"I do, but if he hurts you, I'll bite him without remorse." She snapped her fangs.

"I appreciate the moral support, but I trust Daniel. What we have is true love."

"Yes, yes. You're both special snowflakes and your love will blow the curse to smithereens. Yada yada." She rolled her eyes. "I'm parched from all this naiveté. I think I need another drink."

"If true love could break the Spellbound curse, then it should have been broken when Daniel and I kissed after I ruined his wedding."

Her smile broadened. "That was an excellent day. Such drama."

"It was terrible day with a happy outcome," I corrected her.

"Whatever. So you don't think true love will break the curse. What's left?"

I couldn't breathe a word about the summoning and its implications. Not yet.

"I don't think it's as simple as that, no." I finished my drink. "Anyway, I thought we were going to talk about my mother today."

Catherine returned to the bar for another drink. "Talk

away. I'm listening." She paused. "Wait. Which mother are we discussing?"

"Biological."

"Right." She motioned with her hand. "Carry on."

"So I've been trying to figure out why she would have left me in the care of my parents. With the Harts. What was she afraid of?"

"And you think those letters you saw in your memory might contain clues?"

"I hope so. As far as I know, they're the only link to my mother that exist."

"Any luck manifesting them here?"

"Not yet, but I'm still working on it with Lady Weatherby and Agnes."

"Those two must be a barrel full of pixies."

"They've been very helpful," I said. "And Agnes can be quite entertaining in her own way."

"I'll bet. That witch is psychotic. I wasn't the least bit surprised when her daughter turned out to be a straight arrow. Had to be a complete defense mechanism."

"Okay, enough about Lady Weatherby's mother. Can we get back to mine? I'm nearly out of time."

Catherine consulted the clock on the wall. "So you are. Go on. You've got another minute or so."

I heaved a sigh. "I'd like to know why my mother—my adoptive mother—didn't want my birth mother to come and see me. She seemed to think it would bring danger to us."

"And maybe it did. Your mother died under mysterious circumstances."

"She drowned."

"And she was a witch. She would have known better than to be near water."

"Yes," I said softly. It was difficult to accept that my

biological mother might have played a role in my mother's death, inadvertently or otherwise.

"I'll say this much," Catherine said. "Your mother, the Hart witch, knew what she was signing up for when she took you in. That much seems clear. She knew the risks and made the decision to love you and raise you anyway. There's no reason for you to feel guilty for that."

I clasped my hands in my lap. Catherine was right. I'd been harboring guilt without realizing it. "But if someone murdered her because of me, then it's my fault."

"No, it isn't," Catherine said. "And if you were the reason, then why were you still living with your father afterward? You didn't move, did you?"

I shook my head. "No, my father lost the will to do anything. A move would have been too much effort."

"And yet no one murdered him or came to take you away."

"My father died in an accident," I said. "At least that's what I've always believed. Then I went to live with his parents." Maybe I'd never know what really happened or why. I hated the uncertainty of it all.

Catherine clapped her hands. "That's all we have time for today."

"Ugh. We really need to extend our sessions," I said.

"Not today," she said. "I'm meeting Lewis for a bite to eat and, hopefully, dessert."

"Please mean actual dessert and not a euphemism."

Catherine tilted her head. "What if the whipped cream is on him? Does that count as actual dessert or a euphemism?" She flicked her fingers. "Who cares, right? Besides, if you lick it off a body, the calories don't count."

"That's...not true."

"What would you know about it, prude?" She threw her

head back and laughed. "By the devil, I love our sessions. See you next week, doll."

After therapy, I joined Astrid at the Spellbound Care Home to follow up with the wereweasel, Gene Sutcliffe. When Astrid stopped in the hallway to use the restroom, I took the opportunity to say hello to Agnes in her room. She sat at the small table by the window where I'd first met her, shuffling a deck of cards.

"Good afternoon, dearie," she said without looking at me. "Today's not your usual day."

"I'm not here for training," I said. "Astrid and I are here to speak to Gene Sutcliffe, but she needed the bathroom. Sometimes those lattes go right through you."

The elderly witch remained focused on her cards. "I assume it's something to do with Titus."

"I can't really tell you that," I said.

"I'll remember that the next time you want confidential information from me."

"While we're sort of on the topic, do you know anything about their competitive rivalry?" I queried.

She smirked. "Nope. I'll not say a word."

I placed my hands on my hips. "Is this because I haven't brought you any contraband?"

Agnes gave a small shrug. "Maybe. Maybe not."

I looked at Agnes hunched over her cards, and a memory of Sadie in the cemetery flashed in my mind. "Out of curiosity, has your daughter been to visit you lately? Not counting our training sessions, of course."

"Here and there," Agnes said. "Obviously not as much as I would like, but it's a start."

Her response made me feel a little better. I hated the idea of Agnes dying unexpectedly when she and Lady Weatherby were on bad terms. Those types of gaps needed to be bridged *before* death. Afterward was pretty close to impossible unless you were lucky enough to be a ghost like Gareth and Raisa.

"I spoke to Phoebe Minor recently. She said she was here to see Silas."

Agnes scowled. "That second rate harpy. What a nerve she has coming here. She's got her own home full of old people to wander around in. There's no reason for her to be hanging around my turf."

That was pretty much the reaction I expected. Agnes liked Silas far more than she was willing to admit.

"Did you check whether the bird woman had any interaction with Titus during her visit?" Agnes asked, in a clear effort to throw Phoebe under the bus. "That harpy's such an easy one to irritate. It would have been easy for Titus to get on her bad side quickly."

I sighed. "Agnes, you know perfectly well that Phoebe had no hand in his death. Even if they had experienced some sort of dispute, Phoebe Minor would never murder someone in such a cowardly way. She'd scratch his eyes out with her harpy claws before she'd stoop to potion."

"Fair point," Agnes grumbled.

"Phoebe's like you," I said. "She isn't known for being subtle. She'd go full harpy and ask questions later."

Agnes seemed to consider my statement. "You're right, dearie. She is like me, which is exactly why that genie fancies her."

What Agnes lacked in looks, she made up for in ego. "I bet you're right," I said.

Astrid appeared in the doorway. "How's it going, Agnes?"

"I'm an old witch in a care home. How do you think it's going?"

"You don't need to get snippy with Astrid," I said. "She's only being polite. Something you could use a lesson on."

"It's also polite to bring a gift when you pay someone a visit," Agnes said pointedly.

A-ha! I knew she cared about the absence of contraband. "Well, as I told you, I'm here to see someone else today," I said. "Besides, you're not a hostess. This isn't your house."

She slapped a card on the table. "Speaking of houses, you need to keep an eye on one of yours."

My brow wrinkled. "One of mine? What do you mean? I only have one house."

Agnes tapped the card in front of her. "I'm not talking about a literal house, my dear. I'm talking about your first house. Identity."

I folded my arms across my chest. "You're reading my cards without my permission again? I've asked you before not to do that."

"And you know the more you tell me not to do something, the more likely I am to do it," Agnes said.

"Because you're a toddler in the body of an ancient witch," I snapped.

Agnes gave a soft cackle. "More like a teenager than a toddler, dearie. I've got the boobs to prove it."

I pretended to peer at her. "Those are boobs? And here I thought the care home had a mosquito problem."

Agnes shot me a threatening look.

"We should get going," Astrid said, nudging my shoulder. "The fairy in reception has us on some kind of timer."

Agnes blew a raspberry. "Give me a wand and I'll take care of her for you."

I covered my eyes with my hands. "Agnes, you really need to not make statements like that to the sheriff."

"It's a good thing you're coming to see Gene between meals," she said. "He gets cranky when he's hungry."

"Something you have in common," I yelled, as Astrid dragged me around the corner.

We walked to the adjacent wing of the building where Gene's room was located. The wereweasel was in bed, reading a book. It took me a moment to realize why the image seemed so odd. Then I realized—it was the first time I'd seen one of the residents with a book.

"Gene Sutcliffe?" Astrid said.

He glanced up from his book and smiled when he saw the two of us framed in his doorway.

"And what have I done to deserve two beautiful young ladies in my bedroom? Or have I died and gone to heaven?"

"I'm Sheriff Astrid," the Valkyrie said, ignoring his comment. "And this is my consultant, Emma Hart."

Gene closed the book and set it on his bedside table. "Let me guess. You're here to talk to me about that crotchety old satyr."

We moved further into the room. "That's right," Astrid said. "What makes you think we'd want to talk to you?"

Gene grinned. "The Great Tiddlywinks Argument was rather a big deal when it happened. I'm pretty sure everyone in the care home has heard the story by now."

"Well, we'd like to hear your version of events," Astrid said.

Gene clasped his hands together on his stomach. "It's a simple story, really. Titus accused me of cheating at tiddly-winks and threw an absolute pixie fit. I'm pretty sure he yelled at me for a good twenty minutes straight. Got all red in the face and everything."

"And what did you do?" I asked. "You just let him yell at you?"

Gene shrugged. "I found it entertaining. Besides, it wore him out. I'm pretty sure he napped for an hour afterward. I figure I did the staff a favor. Most of them couldn't stand him."

So Gene considered himself a hero. How far would a hero be willing to go to please his admirers?

"We noticed that a Franklin Sutcliffe came to see you the day of the murder," Astrid said. "Any relation?"

"My son," Gene replied. "He's a regular visitor. He was far less entertained by Titus than I was. Franklin's easily offended, though, especially when it comes to accusations of cheating." Gene swung his legs over the side of the bed. "We're wereweasels, you know? We have certain sensitivities."

I raised my hand. "I have a question."

"You were a good student, weren't you?" Gene asked. "Good students always raise their hands. So polite and patient."

"I did reasonably well." I wasn't about to give him my GPA, not that the number would mean anything in Spellbound.

He winked. "So what's your question, pretty lady?"

"Was Titus telling the truth? Did you cheat?" I asked.

A slow smile emerged. "'Course I did. You should've seen the look on that satyr's face. Oh, it was priceless."

"So you let everyone believe that you'd been wrongly accused?" Astrid asked, her outrage evident.

"Had to for the good of the species," Gene said. "Franklin would've been horrified if I'd admitted the truth." He inclined his head toward me. "He dates one of yours. A witch called Jemima."

I nearly choked. "Jemima?" That was news to me. How anyone could tolerate Jemima for more than five minutes was beyond me.

"That's right. He brought her here a couple of weeks ago. Such a proud fella. Wanted to show off his new girl. Franklin's always wanted to fit in. Wereweasels tend to be ostracized, even among shifters. That's why he was so offended by Titus."

"Did he do anything about it?" I asked. "Like speak to a member of staff?"

"Doubtful," Gene said. "Franklin doesn't like confrontation. He's got the sneaky weasel DNA. He'd piss in Titus's pudding or something and watch him eat it."

Ew. "Or maybe put Organ Massacre in his drink?"

Gene's expression darkened. "No way. Not Franklin."

"How about you?" Astrid asked.

Gene chuckled. "How would I even get access to a potion like Organ Massacre? I don't leave the building. Besides, I told you already—I wasn't upset about it."

"Because you had, in fact, cheated," I said.

The wereweasel touched the end of his nose with his index finger. "Precisely."

CHAPTER 10

STONE WALLS SURROUNDED me and the air was damp and chilly. This place seemed familiar, yet I couldn't remember why. When I spotted a woman with golden blond hair seated in front of a small fire on the ground, my stomach lurched. I knew exactly where I was. I'd had this dream before, or some semblance of it. Why was I having the dream again?

I walked toward the woman, less frightened than I'd been the first time. "Hello," I said. "I'm Emma."

The figure ignored me.

"Can you hear me?" I asked.

The woman murmured to herself as she ripped off leaves from a plant and chucked them into the flames. It seemed to be the same incantation as the last time I'd been here. I moved to the other side of the fire to get a better view of her. Her skin was as smooth as I remembered and her stark white eyes every bit as unnerving.

I listened again to the incantation but still couldn't make out the words, other than a few Latin ones here and there. Not enough to piece anything together. I wasn't Laurel.

The bits of plants and herbs exploded in the flames, same

as before. The woman bowed her head, the incantation complete.

"I'd like to know why I'm back here," I said loudly. "You must be important, but I don't know why."

The woman didn't acknowledge me. I glanced around the stone room to see there was still no entrance or exit. Colorful remnants of the explosion drifted through the air and moved to the perimeter, where the wall disintegrated. Instead of being transported to an open field like before, we stood in a clearing in the middle of a forest. The woman stretched her arms toward the sun and closed her eyes. Golden rays of light the color of her hair shimmered through the trees. I felt a momentary sense of calm, until the beams of golden light hardened. I twisted and turned, watching as they drove into the ground around us and formed a circle. My heart pounded in my chest. I was trapped inside a golden prison with the mysterious, white-eyed woman.

The ground rumbled beneath my feet and I screamed as the forest floor disintegrated. I clutched at anything and everything around me—rocks, bushes, vines, but my fingers slipped through empty air. Above me I heard the woman's loud and high cackle—the one that made my blood run cold. I was falling, falling...

"Emma." Gareth's concerned voice cut through my scream. "Emma, wake up."

My eyes flew open and I struggled to focus on my roommate.

"You look like you've seen a ghost," he said.

"I'm seeing one right now."

He chuckled. "I suppose so. What were you dreaming about?"

I sat up and felt my pulse begin to slow. "It was another nightmare. Same wild lady with the awful laugh."

Gareth continued to hover beside the bed. "Still no idea who she is?"

"Nope. She trapped me in the forest this time and then the ground fell away."

"You should tell Dr. Hall about it," he said.

"I will at my next appointment." I threw back the covers and got out of bed. "It's probably anxiety."

A tap on the window startled me. Sedgwick turned his head one hundred eighty degrees to view the source of the sound. Another owl stared back at him.

"Friend of his?" Gareth mused, looking at Sedgwick.

"That's the coven owl," I said. I crossed the room to open the window and retrieved a message from the owl's beak. "Thank you."

The owl flew off and I closed the window. "There's an emergency meeting they want me to attend."

"About the parchment?" Gareth queried. I'd told Gareth since, of course, he couldn't tell anyone.

"I guess so. Better get dressed."

"Wear something conservative," he said. "And don't forget your cloak."

"According to you, all my clothes are conservative."

"True. Wear your navy blue dress. That makes you look like you came over on the Mayflower."

I squinted at him. "Do I want to look like a Pilgrim for the coven meeting?"

He shrugged. "It wouldn't hurt."

I hurried to shower and dress and drove Sigmund into town. The other remedial witches were already waiting outside the meeting room when I arrived.

"You look nervous," Millie said to me. "Did you take your anti-anxiety potion this morning?"

"I didn't have time," I said. "I woke up from a nightmare and then the owl arrived with the message."

Begonia squeezed my hand. "Please don't puke on anyone."

The door opened and Meg gestured for us to enter.

"Good morning, witches," Professor Holmes said. "Won't you all have a seat and we'll get started?"

We crammed into the empty seats at the oversized table. The space was designed more like a conference room than the Great Hall. A less formal set-up suited me just fine.

Lady Weatherby sat at the head of the table, while Meg took her place between Ginger and Professor Holmes.

"We've deliberately kept this meeting small," Lady Weatherby informed us. "We only want to thank you all in person for your incredible discovery." She shifted her focus to me. "Miss Hart, you should know that I am presenting the information to the council with the coven's recommendation that you perform the summoning and retrieve the horn."

I didn't know whether to cheer or vomit. Both responses seemed equally appropriate.

"That's terrific," Begonia blurted.

"We'd also like you to continue decoding the remainder of the parchment," Professor Holmes said. "We had a runecraft lesson on the schedule for next month, but this is a much better way to learn and far more urgent in nature."

"Real world application always provides a better learning experience," Meg agreed. "And we so rarely have the opportunity to provide it."

"Are you sure about me?" I asked. Now that I had their support, I was beginning to waver. What if I messed up the summoning and ruined everyone's chances to break the curse?

Professor Holmes's kindly eyes twinkled. "Emma, my dear, we've always been sure about you."

"Once the council renders its decision, the coven will

assist you in preparing," Lady Weatherby said. "Your sorceress training will need to be put on hold."

"Of course. The summoning takes priority." Although Agnes would be disappointed, I knew she'd understand.

"Do you have any questions?" Professor Holmes asked.

I hesitated. "If I fail, does that mean we lose our chance to get the horn forever? Or would someone else be able to perform the summoning for another shot?"

Lady Weatherby's expression gave nothing away. "We are uncertain at this point. The parchment is unclear."

So it was a risk. If I screwed up the summoning, we may never get another chance to get the horn.

My palms began to sweat. "If I don't manage to get the horn, is it possible there are other spells out there to break the curse?"

"Calm down, Emma," Ginger said in a soothing tone. "Try not to put too much pressure on yourself."

"How can I not?" I asked. It seemed that the fate of the entire town rested on my narrow shoulders.

Ginger gave me a sympathetic look. "The truth is we don't know if there's another spell out there. It's certainly possible. In fact, the coven has been working on that assumption for years."

"There's more than one way to skin a snake," Professor Holmes said.

I blinked. "Isn't it 'to skin a cat'?"

"Bite your tongue," Lady Weatherby said, with an exaggerated nod toward Chairman Meow. I hadn't even noticed the cat on the floor beside her.

"Sorry," I mumbled.

"We don't know who drafted the paper you found," Meg added. "Nor do we know why it was hidden."

"And right now it doesn't matter," Lady Weatherby said. "Right now the priority is to successfully complete the summoning and retrieve the horn. Once the council has rendered its decision on your participation, I shall send for you."

"How soon?" I asked.

"I've called an emergency meeting to discuss the matter," she said. "How long it will take to decide the issue is up to the council members. Certain members have a tendency to debate issues *ad nauseam*. I'm sure you can guess which ones they are."

I held my tongue. I had no desire to bad mouth council members in front of one of the council's more esteemed members. At least Lucy was on the council now that she was the mayor. With Lady Weatherby and Lucy, that was two votes right there. My panic began to subside.

"As a token of our appreciation for all of your efforts," Professor Holmes began, "we have decided to cancel classes this week. You may enjoy an unscheduled holiday from the academy."

I stifled the loud cheer that bubbled up in my throat. Probably best not to show too much enthusiasm. My friends seemed to have the same thought because they continued to sit quietly at the table, though I was certain I felt their excited vibes.

"You are dismissed," Lady Weatherby said, and Chairman Meow swished his tail for good measure.

With classes cancelled, I opted to make an appearance in my lately-ignored office. At the very least, it would be nice to chat with Althea without a court case hanging over my head.

"I was hoping you'd pop in today," Althea said, opening our adjoining door.

"Because you missed my smiling face?" I stopped short when I noticed her somber expression. "What's the matter?"

She drew a steadying breath. "Remember your plant?"

Instinctively, I glanced at the empty windowsill. "Where is it? Let me guess. You've moved it to your office for safe-keeping."

"You know I would never do that. Your office gets better natural light."

I eyed her curiously. "Althea, where's my plant?"

"Dead." Her snakes hissed at the word and she quieted them with a gentle pat of her headscarf.

"Oh, no. I'm so sorry. I told you I was terrible keeping things alive."

"It's not your fault," she said. "That's what I need to tell you. The plant was poisoned."

My head jerked toward her. "Poisoned? Why on earth would someone poison my plant?"

"Your guess is as good as mine."

"Who would have access to my office without one of us knowing?" I couldn't come up with a single name.

"No one," she replied. "But it wouldn't be difficult for an experienced magic user to come and go undetected."

I sank into my chair and heaved a sigh. "What's the point? Is it a warning? Is it just to be mean? Was it an accident?" My mind whirred with ideas.

Althea sat in one of the client chairs opposite me. "I wish I knew. Believe me, I have my own beef with the culprit. I've kept that plant alive for years. I'm taking this personally."

"What kind of poison was it?" I asked. "Maybe I should talk to Astrid." The sheriff had bigger fish to fry right now with the satyr's murder, though. She wasn't going to be too bothered by a houseplant.

"It's called Dry Me A River," Althea replied. "Sucks all the moisture out of any living thing."

"So even though we watered the plant, the poison dried it up?"

"Exactly."

I shuddered. "That could turn someone into a husk."

Althea pressed her lips together and nodded. "I didn't want to say it out loud."

My anxiety level began to rise. "What if someone came in here to poison me, but lost their nerve and threw it into the plant?"

"There are a hundred possibilities," Althea said. "Until we figure it out, I think you should put a protective spell around the office just to be on the safe side."

My first thought was of Mayor Knightsbridge. She'd sworn revenge on me for my role in her removal from office. She was under house arrest, but that didn't mean she couldn't find someone to poison me on her behalf.

"I already have a protective spell on my house," I said. Demetrius had taken care of that a while ago. "I'll see about doing one for here."

"Do your car, too," Althea suggested. "And your broomstick. Anything of yours that someone could use against you."

The back of my neck prickled. I wasn't uncomfortable with this turn of events. I generally felt safe in Spellbound, especially in my office. It was another sanctuary for me.

"How about a latte to make you feel better?" Althea asked. "Your usual? I'll run over to Brew-Ha-Ha and get it for you."

"No, thanks. I'm afraid to drink anything right now."

Althea gave me a wry smile. "I'll even take the first sip. Test it for poison."

"Fine," I relented. "I didn't sleep very well with my bad dream last night. A latte is probably a good idea. Have Henrik add a shot of optimism."

"Sounds perfect. I'll do that."

Once Althea left, I tried to keep my mind occupied. I took out my quill and parchment and began to write down everything I knew about the murder of Titus. Even though he'd been unpopular and there were plenty of motives for murder, I still couldn't pinpoint an obvious suspect. This seemed to be one of those cases where there were too many aggrieved paranormals in the mix.

My gaze flickered to the empty windowsill and I couldn't help but worry about the poisoned plant. Was I destined to end up like Titus? Would Astrid be making a list of suspects for my murder next? It wasn't like anyone *planned* to be murdered. It could happen to anyone at any time. I shivered and tried to focus on the satyr. Holy anxiety, I needed that shot of optimism pronto.

The door opened and I was about to remark on Althea's speed when I noticed Astrid in the doorway.

"Hey, I wasn't expecting you," I said.

"I saw Althea and she said you were here. I'm heading over to interview Deanna, Titus's former partner. Turns out she's the sole beneficiary of the will. Wanna come?"

"Desperately." Anything to take my mind off my own problems.

"It's a short walk," she said. "Deanna works at Paws and Claws."

"Perfect. Then I'll grab my latte from Althea on the way."

Paws and Claws was the animal rescue center where I'd met Sedgwick. I'd gone there expecting to come home with a cat as my familiar like all the other witches in town. Instead I ended up with a cantankerous owl. That should've been my first clue that I wasn't a typical witch.

Astrid and I located Deanna in a section of the room with about twenty meowing cats. They circled around her like she was telling them a story. The scene reminded me more of a daycare than an animal rescue center.

"Deanna?" Astrid queried.

The older elf glanced up from her feline companions. "Yes, that's me. Hello, Sheriff. And I recognize you, Emma Hart."

"You do?" It never ceased to amaze me that Spellbound residents recognized me. Although my hometown of Lemon Grove, Pennsylvania was relatively small, people didn't recognize me the way they did here. Then again, I wasn't a sorceress back in Lemon Grove. I was a busy lawyer with a lot of bills and very little time to socialize.

"Of course," Deanna said. "It's not every day Spellbound gets a new resident, unless someone gives birth."

"Were you here the day I met Sedgwick?" I didn't remember her.

She smiled. "I was. You probably didn't notice me. I believe I was knee-deep in litter boxes at the time. I remember being so surprised that the new witch left with an owl instead of a cat."

"You and me both," I replied.

"I've matched many coven members with their familiars over the years," she said. "It's one of the most rewarding parts of the job."

"Do you have a few minutes to talk?" Astrid asked.

"Yes, of course. I'm simply telling the cats the story about Puss-in-Boots. They like to hear about their heroes."

It was hard to view Deanna through the same lens as Sadie. The petite elf seemed so likable and genuine—not the satyr-stealing temptress that Sadie described.

"Have you heard the news about Titus?" Astrid asked.

Deanna's expression clouded over. "He's dead, isn't he?"

Astrid's ears perked up. "What makes you say that?"

"For one thing, he's old. Older than me. For another thing, he's been living in the Spellbound Care Home for years. I can't imagine he was happy. He probably died just to get out of there."

"Actually, he was murdered," Astrid said.

Wow, she was busting out the big guns right from the get-go.

Deanna's brow lifted. She seemed genuinely surprised by the news. "Why would someone murder Titus?"

"We were hoping you could help us with that," I said. "His daughter tells us that you and Titus were in a serious relationship for many years."

Deanna closed her eyes and swallowed hard. "Sadie."

"Yes, Sadie." I waited to see whether the older elf would say more.

"She still hates me, doesn't she?" Deanna asked. She crouched on the floor to pet one of the cats. I suspected the gesture was more comforting for the elf than the cat.

"Sadie's feelings are irrelevant," Astrid said. "We're just trying to get to the bottom of Titus's murder."

Deanna pressed her lips together. "Did she try to blame me for the murder? Is that why you're here now?"

"We're here now because you had a prior relationship with the victim and you may have information that's helpful to the investigation," Astrid said. "That's all."

Deanna stroked another cat. "I'm not sure how I can help you. Titus and I haven't been together in a number of years. We weren't good about staying in touch. Too difficult...for both of us."

"When was the last time you saw him?" Astrid asked.

"I honestly don't remember," she replied. "We were separated by the time he moved into the care home and I only went to visit him once or twice after that." She paused, remembering. "I felt guilty, but my relationship with him cost me too much. I had to stop communicating with him."

"What do you mean?" I asked. As far as I knew, Deanna had been unattached when she got involved with Titus. It was the satyr who'd had a partner and daughter.

Deanna sat on the floor and let a few of the cats settle on her lap. "When Titus and I first got involved, we were very much in love. We knew that we hurt others, but we believed the outcome was worth the pain we'd caused. After a couple of years, the guilt crept in."

"His or yours?" I queried.

"Both," she said. "He wasn't spending the time with his daughter that he should've been, and I blamed myself for that. Every time I urged him to see her, he would lose his temper with me. Then, in the next breath, he would blame me for their estrangement."

"Sadie still seems to blame you," Astrid said. "To be fair, though, she blames her father equally."

Deanna nodded, tears glistening in her eyes. "I would have welcomed her into our home, but her mother hated both of us with such intensity… She never would've allowed it. And I didn't want to drive a wedge between Sadie and her mother after being the reason her father left in the first place."

I felt sorry for Deanna. She seemed like a nice woman who had been in a tough spot. "How did you meet Titus?"

"I met him here," she said, smiling happily. "He'd come in to find a pet for Sadie's birthday. Sadie's mother objected, but he was determined to give his little girl what she wanted. I was impressed with his dedication. It was foolish of me, though. I should have recognized the selfishness of his act. Sadie's mother had her reasons, yet he ignored them so that he could be the hero."

"It sounds like he stopped playing the hero for his daughter," I said. For everyone, really. At some point, Titus wandered into grumpy old man territory and never returned.

Deanna's shoulders tensed. "That's true. Once we met, he seemed to transfer all his energy to me. I was flattered, of course. We both fell hard and fast. After that, it didn't take him long to leave his partner."

"Since you didn't know he was dead, I guess no one's contacted you about his will," Astrid said.

Deanna shook her head. "I can't imagine he had much. I hope Sadie gets something to remember him by."

Astrid and I exchanged uncomfortable glances.

"Actually, he left everything to you," Astrid said.

Deanna choked back tears. "Why would he do that? We haven't spoken for years."

"In his own way, he still loved you," I said. Inasmuch as it was possible for a miserable, selfish satyr to love someone.

Deanna squeezed her eyes closed. "He shouldn't have done that. He should've left it all to Sadie. It was the one thing he could've done to make up for the pain he caused her."

"I'm told he could be quite disagreeable," I said. "It doesn't sound like he was concerned about making up for bad behavior."

A soft breath escaped her lips. "No, his selfishness was one of the reasons we didn't last. So many times, I forgave him and went back to him. He couldn't change, though. Didn't want to. I finally had to put an end to it to save my sanity. We weren't healthy together. I don't think Titus was capable of having a healthy relationship with anyone. There's a part of me that thinks Sadie was better off without him in her life."

"I think Sadie would disagree with that," I said.

"That's only because she didn't know him," Deanna said. Gently, she removed the cats from her lap and stood. "How did he die?"

"A poisonous potion called Organ Massacre," Astrid said.

"Was it painful?" she asked.

Astrid hesitated. "Most likely it was."

Deanna's face tightened and I could see her struggling to keep a lid on her emotions. Unlike Sadie, she clearly didn't want him to have suffered.

"I'm sorry I couldn't be more helpful," Deanna said. "I hope you catch whoever did this. I know he wasn't...I know he let everyone down and could be difficult, but he had a lot of love inside, too. It was just really hard to get to it. Like a thick wall of ice, you had to keep chipping away over time." She blinked away tears. "You had to really want access to it. Most folks don't have the patience for it."

"You should talk to Stan about Titus's will," Astrid said.

"Stan's the town registrar," I added.

Deanna dried her cheeks. "Do you think Sadie would object if I gave her whatever was left in the estate?" She gave a quick shake of her head. "No. She probably wouldn't want to hear from me. Not now."

I placed a hand on Deanna's shoulder. "It would be a nice gesture, but don't expect miracles. Sadie still carries around a lot of pain and bitterness."

"I don't blame her," Deanna said. She drew a deep breath. "But I'd like to try. I owe her that much."

"Good luck, Deanna," I said. "I'm sorry for your loss."

Deanna offered a sad sigh. "Thank you, but the truth is I lost him a long time ago."

CHAPTER 11

BETWEEN MY POISONED PLANT, the coven meeting, and Deanna's interview, I was emotionally spent by the time evening rolled around. The only thing I wanted to do was climb under the covers and shove a pillow over my head.

"Company's here," Gareth said, as I spit out my toothpaste. "I opened the door for them."

I knew it wasn't Daniel because he was volunteering at the care home tonight. He was serving as referee for the indoor pool games, including one called canoe fight where two groups of residents tried to sink the other party's canoe. I stayed away from water-related activities because of my longstanding fear of drowning, not to mention I was currently burned out on care home visits.

"It's Sophie and the miserable one," Gareth said.

"Millie."

"Aye. Magpie has gone to greet them."

I rinsed my mouth one more time before running downstairs. Letting Magpie greet my guests was never a good idea.

"Magpie, back away slowly," I called. He was blocking

their path to the staircase by hissing and giving them the stink eye.

The cat turned and gave me the same treatment.

"Hey," I objected. "I live here, remember? If it weren't for me, you'd be hunting and gathering in the forest for food."

Magpie's tail swished left and right. He refused to acknowledge my role in his comfort. No matter. I didn't have the energy to argue with the beast from hell. I directed my attention to my friends. At least they wouldn't give me attitude. Okay, maybe Millie would.

"What's up?" I asked.

"We're going to the Horned Owl and you're coming with us," Sophie said.

"No, I'm not," I said. "I'm ready for bed."

"Sophie is desperate to see Ty, and I'm not getting stuck as the third wheel," Millie said.

"Where's Begonia?" I asked.

Millie gave me a knowing look. "Where do you think?"

"Demetrius?"

They nodded.

"Please come," Sophie begged. "We don't have classes this week. I just want to go out and have fun." When she flashed her puppy dog eyes, I knew I was doomed. I had a weakness for puppy dog eyes.

"Let me get changed and run a brush through this mess," I said, touching my head. "It looks like Sedgwick got his claws caught in my hair."

"I'm glad you said it," Gareth quipped from the top of the steps.

The Horned Owl was so packed when we arrived, I was convinced there was a special event that no one told me about.

"What's the big attraction tonight?" Millie asked Ty as we stepped up to the bar. It wasn't easy to get a spot, but Millie had devised a simple spell that moved people a couple of inches to the side. It didn't seem like a useful spell until you were standing in the middle of a crowd. I told her she should have used that spell for her advanced project instead of the ideal beauty necklace.

"There's a band tonight," Ty said. "They've acquired quite a following, it seems."

"Who's the band?" Sophie asked, her eyes shining brightly. She looked so pleased to see Ty—it was just the heart-warming moment I needed to lift my spirits.

The satyr smiled at the sight of her. "Hi, Sophie. You look pretty tonight."

"Thank you," Sophie replied. "So do you." She frowned. "I mean, not pretty…"

Ty laughed. "I'll take the compliment. It's not every day a horned guy like me gets called pretty." He poured three cock-tails and slid them across the bar. "The band is called Nameless Faces. You should hang around for a listen."

Sophie nodded enthusiastically and glanced our way for confirmation.

"I can't stay out too late," I said. "I need a decent night's sleep for a change."

"You should go back to harp therapy," Sophie suggested.

Britta and me both, I thought to myself.

"Drink those fast so you can come back for more," Ty said, his gaze pinned on Sophie. "Not too fast, though." He seemed to realize his error. "I mean, you need to drink responsibly."

I smothered a laugh. "Of course."

We took our drinks and went in search of a table. No easy feat when every booth was taken.

"Millie, do you know any more useful spells to clear out a booth?" Sophie asked.

Millie surveyed the pub, her gaze settling on a table of drunken werewolves. One was nearly passed out on his friend's shoulder.

"I think I can do something about them," she said smugly.

"I don't think getting them to move a couple of inches to the side is going to be of any use," I said. "They'll still be in the booth." Or on the floor next to the booth.

Millie retrieved her wand and discreetly pointed it in the direction of the table. She murmured a spell under her breath, and, before I knew it, the werewolves shot out of their seats and out of the pub altogether. We slipped into the booth without any trouble.

Sophie stared at Millie in amazement. "Which spell was that?"

Millie steepled her fingers on the table in a gesture that reminded me of Lady Weatherby. "I call it the whistle spell."

"Like a dog whistle?" Sophie queried.

Millie nodded. "It's a distraction technique. They think they heard it outside, so they go to investigate. They can't help themselves."

"Does it only work on werewolves?" I asked.

"So far," Millie said. "To be honest, I haven't had many chances to test it yet. This was a perfect opportunity."

We sipped our cocktails and I watched as Sophie exchanged flirtatious glances with Ty.

I nudged her with my elbow. "Why don't you just go sit at the bar and talk to him? Millie and I don't mind."

"Speak for yourself," said Millie. "She needs to at least spend five minutes with us. Next thing you know, she'll be like Begonia and ditching us at every opportunity."

I debated whether to tell my friends what I'd witnessed when I trailed Demetrius the other night. In the end, I opted for secrecy. I didn't need to give Millie another reason to resent Demetrius. Until I had more facts, I didn't want to say or do anything that hurt Begonia's relationship with them. With so many investigations going at once, I needed more hours in the day.

"I'll finish my drink with you two and then I'll go talk to Ty," Sophie said. "He's so busy with this crowd anyway. I don't want to be in the way."

"Based on the way he looked at you," I said, "he wants you in the way."

Sophie's cheeks grew flushed.

"You must be nervous about the council meeting," Millie said. "I passed Maeve McCullen on her way to the Great Hall."

My eyes widened. "They're meeting tonight?"

Millie nodded. "No one told you?"

I sucked down more of my drink. "No, but I guess there's no need until the matter's been discussed. They'll call me in front of the council once they've made their decision."

"We're here to support you," Sophie said. "Don't let the summoning stress you out."

"Unfortunately, I've got more on my mind than just the summoning," I said, and told them about my poisoned plant.

"Who would do that?" Sophie asked, aghast.

"I bet it's one of Mayor Knightsbridge's cronies," Millie said.

"That was my first thought," I admitted. "Well, I guess the good news is that if the council decides to let me do the summoning, there's a chance I won't survive. Whomever's trying to hurt me or scare me can let a unicorn do the dirty work."

Sophie shot me a sympathetic look. "Nothing bad is going to happen, Emma. It may be challenging, but a sacred unicorn won't want to kill you. They're docile creatures."

I smiled. "I'll try to remember that when I'm getting staked by a golden horn."

"Oh no," Millie said. "Don't look now, but Jemima is here and I think she's spotted us."

"Really?" I craned my neck for a better view. "Where is she? I actually need to speak to her."

Millie balked. "Since when do you want to talk to Jemima? She's awful."

"Yes, but she's also dating Franklin Sutcliffe," I said.

"Who's Franklin Sutcliffe?" Sophie asked.

"His father is a resident in the care home." I didn't want to say much more than that.

"Is this about the murder?" Sophie asked.

"I can neither confirm nor deny." I took another sip of my drink. Ty seemed to be making them stronger than usual tonight. I'd have to make sure I didn't have too many.

Sure enough, Jemima threaded her way through the crowd to our table. The man beside her was unmistakably the son of Gene Sutcliffe. They had the same tiny round eyes and reedy frame. Whereas Gene had a full mustache and beard, Franklin only had what appeared to be a sickly caterpillar growing above his upper lip. For a moment, I wondered what Jemima saw in him, but then I realized that the better question was—what did Franklin see in Jemima?

"What do we have here?" Jemima asked, sidling up to the table. Her high-pitched voice alone made my skin crawl. "Only three remedial witches tonight? Have you lost one or two along the way?"

"You know perfectly well that Laurel is too young to be here," Millie said.

"And Begonia is out with her boyfriend," I said. "I'm sure you know Demetrius Hunt." Everyone knew the sexy vampire. I had no doubt that Jemima was green with envy over Begonia's relationship with him.

"Yes, I heard they've been seen around town together," Jemima said. "I guess she doesn't mind sharing him with the succubus he's also been spotted with."

The other girls exchanged confused glances.

"Begonia knows all about Marcie," I lied. "She doesn't mind because her relationship with Demetrius is secure." I smiled at Franklin. "And you must be Jemima's lucky boyfriend."

Jemima linked her arm through his. "How rude of me. Girls, this is Franklin Sutcliffe. We met at Monte Carlo Night at the country club last month."

Hmm. They only met last month. What if Franklin's whole purpose in meeting her was to gain access to the ingredients for Organ Massacre? I took the opportunity to dig for information. "Sutcliffe? Are you related to Gene, by any chance?"

Franklin smiled. "He's my father."

I finished off my drink. "He's quite the entertaining wereweasel. I met him recently when I was visiting a friend in the care home."

Jemima rolled her eyes. "You're not still spending time there with that crone, Agnes, are you?"

"Agnes has been an incredible help to me," I said. I wanted Jemima to be quiet, so that I could keep the conversation going with Franklin. "Do you visit your father often? I'm sure I would remember you if we'd run into one another in the hall."

"I'm there every Tuesday and Thursday," Franklin said. "Dad and I play cards or hang out in the games room. He really likes it there."

Out of the corner of my eye, I noticed the band beginning to set up on a makeshift platform. I hoped the music wasn't so loud that I couldn't continue my interrogation…er, conversation.

"Terrible news about Titus, though," I said, regarding him carefully.

His face looked blank. "Titus?" He snapped his fingers. "Oh, the grumpy dude. Yeah, Dad wasn't a fan of his."

I leaned forward. "No? Any particular reason?"

"They were competitive with each other," Franklin said. "Titus liked to accuse my dad of cheating."

"That must have been upsetting," I said.

Franklin scowled. "Not for my dad, but it bugged me. We're wereweasels. We already have a certain unfair reputation. Calling my dad a cheater plays into the stereotype. It's racist."

I hadn't really thought about it that way. "I can understand why that would bother you."

Jemima rubbed his arm. "Franklin's idea of being upset is sulking on the sofa. He's the complete opposite of me."

No doubt.

"You ladies look like you're in need of another drink," Franklin said. "Can I buy the next round?"

"I wouldn't object to that," Millie said.

Franklin glanced at Jemima. "And how about you, honey bunny? Same drink?"

Jemima batted her eyelashes so furiously, it looked like she was fighting off some kind of particle invasion. "Yes, my darling."

Sophie choked back a groan.

"I'll be right back," Franklin said and disappeared into the crowd.

I appealed straight to Jemima's vanity. "How did you snag that one? He seems wonderful."

Jemima hugged herself. "He is. I can hardly believe my luck. He approached me at the country club, like I said. I was at the roulette table and he asked if I'd be interested in taking a chance on him. Isn't that romantic?

Either romantic or very calculated. "He doesn't mind that you're a witch?" I queried. I knew some species were particular about partners in other paranormal communities. Shifters in particular seemed to want to stick together.

"It was just the opposite, in fact. He seemed genuinely intrigued. He loves me to show off my magic." Jemima exhaled happily. "I still pinch myself every morning."

Well, she certainly did seem smitten. If Franklin had wanted something from her in the potion shop, I had no doubt he could wrangle it from her.

"I bet he dotes on you. Visits you at work and brings you coffee and treats," I said, smiling. "Gotta love the honeymoon phase."

Jemima nodded enthusiastically. "Almost every day. A couple of times he's been mistaken for an employee. I told him he needs to stop spending so much time there." She laughed.

"I would think he'd get bored," Millie said. "Shifters don't know anything about potions."

"That's one thing I love about Franklin," she said. "He's interested in everything I do. He's always asking questions. He's so smart and funny."

As my grandfather used to say, there's a pipe for every smoker.

Franklin returned with Teena, one of the servers, carrying a tray of drinks behind him. She distributed the drinks with a friendly smile.

"Nice to see you, Ty's magical muffin," Teena said, with a wink at Sophie.

The moment Teena turned away with the empty tray, we burst into laughter.

"Magical muffin sounds like a euphemism for something naughty," I said.

"I definitely haven't done anything naughty with Ty,"

Sophie said. "We can barely get past saying each other's names."

Franklin set his drink on the table and took Jemima by the hand. "A dance, my lady?"

Jemima bumped him with her hip. "Anything for you." She set her glass beside his. "Watch our drinks, witches. My boyfriend wants to dance and dance we shall."

I cringed. Her shrill voice was annoying at the best of times. Throw in a smug attitude and I was ready to hurl.

"Can we mess with their drinks?" Millie pleaded. "One little spell?"

"Absolutely not," I said.

Millie folded her hands together in a pleading gesture. "Pretty please with fairy glitter on top?"

I found myself relenting. "Like what?" I still wanted to keep an eye on Franklin and gauge the type of wereweasel he was. Just because Jemima said his idea of being upset was sitting on the sofa didn't make it true.

"Maybe a little bladder spell on Jemima's drink," Millie said.

I narrowed my eyes. "This reminds me of the time you made my boobs bigger."

"And you never thanked me for that, by the way," Millie said, with a nod toward my chest. "I did you a favor."

"Ha! You're lucky I didn't suffer back strain."

"Millie, you can't do it," Sophie said. "It's the kind of thing Jemima would do. We want to be better than her, right?"

Millie slumped against the back of the booth. "Fine. Let's have integrity. Zzzz." She pretended to fall asleep.

"Good, if Millie's asleep, can I see Ty now?" Sophie asked.

"Go for it," I said. "I'll hold down the fort here."

Millie snapped to attention as Sophie left the booth, drink in hand. "Do you think he'll actually ask her out this time?"

I glanced in the bartender's direction. "I hope so. I don't know what he's waiting for."

"If she weren't so shy, she could ask him," Millie said.

The music grew louder and the band's energy filled the room. "They're very good," I said. "The bass player is cute. What do you think?"

Millie turned around to check out the elf. "The drummer is cuter."

My gaze rested on the beefy guy behind the drum set. "He looks familiar."

"That's Anton," Millie said. "He's a wizard."

"You know him?" I asked.

"He's friends with my oldest brother. They basically ignore me." She shrugged.

I studied Millie. "So, do you have a crush on him?"

Millie polished off her drink. "Maybe. It doesn't matter, though. I'll always be Gabe's little sister."

"Is your brother here?" I didn't notice any wizards tonight.

"Not that I saw. He tends to go to the clubs. He likes to dance with as many girls as he can before curfew. It's like a personal competition."

"We should talk to Anton when they take a break," I suggested.

She rolled her eyes. "Sure, because bands love it when girls rush the stage after a set."

"They kinda do," I said. "Anyway, it's a chance for Anton to see you in a different light."

"I could wear my ideal beauty necklace," Millie said, then frowned. "I'm not sure where it is, actually."

"You don't want to do that," I said. "You want Anton to see *you*, not some distorted version of you."

Millie tapped the rim of her empty glass. "I don't know. Sometimes I think a distorted version would be better."

"Why would you say that?" I mean, Millie could be annoying, but she was no Jemima. She definitely had redeeming qualities.

"Come on," Millie said, mildly exasperated. "I'm not as pretty as any of you. Even Laurel's going to attract more guys than me when she's a couple years older. And I know I can be…difficult sometimes."

I wondered whether it was the alcohol making Millie open up to me. "Millie, you have a beauty that's all your own. Your confidence alone is attractive." Millie's confidence was her main personality trait.

"It isn't as easy for me as it is for you, though," Millie said. "I feel like I have to club guys over the head to notice me."

"I don't recommend it," I said. "Otherwise I'll be defending you in court." I smiled.

"Paranormals don't care about me the way they care about you," Millie complained. "If I had a plant poisoned, they'd wonder what I did to deserve it."

"Millie, that's not true," I objected. "Everyone cares about you, especially our little group."

She blew out a short burst of air. "Oh, please. If you had the chance to ditch me, you absolutely would. I don't bring anything to the group."

I wagged a finger at her. "Now that doesn't sound like the confident Millie I know. You were instrumental in finding the parchment. You helped Laurel with her reveal spell, remember? Without that, we never would've discovered it."

"I guess so." Millie turned around for another brief look at Anton. "Maybe if I was more like you—running around helping everybody all the time like some sort of self-appointed humanitarian—Anton would have noticed me by now."

"You do help others, Millie," I insisted, choosing to ignore the backhanded compliment. "Anyway, you have a warped perception of my ability to attract guys. Remember, you're talking to a grown woman who's still a virgin."

"I assumed that was your choice. You know, like no one's good enough for me."

My mouth dropped open. "It's *not* because I think no one's good enough. It's more because I never had a boyfriend until Daniel. When you lose everyone you love early in life, it makes it difficult to let people in." I finished my second drink and my head began to swim. Definitely time to call it quits. "Believe me, Emma in Spellbound has a far more interesting life than Emma in Lemon Grove ever did."

Millie's mouth quirked. "So maybe I'd be something special in the human world. I hope you break the curse. I hope one day I get the chance to find out."

"Make no mistake, Millie," I said, giving her hand a reassuring squeeze. "You're already something special right here."

CHAPTER 12

THANKFULLY I CHOSE to leave the Horned Owl at a reasonable hour and get a full night's rest because I was summoned before the council early the next morning.

The door to the Great Hall opened and Mayor Langtree's new assistant ushered me in—a werewolf called Nichole. It felt strange to see my friend Lucy where Mayor Knightsbridge used to sit on the dais.

"Welcome back, Miss Hart," Lorenzo Mancini said. The alpha of the werewolf pack was no fan of mine, but at least he had the decency to be polite.

"Take a seat, Emma," Lucy instructed. I could tell she was struggling to strike a balance between friendly and official.

I sat in a chair in the front row, staring down the long table of solemn faces. Although it was hardly my first time in front of the council, I still found the experience to be an intimidating one. These were some of the most powerful and influential residents in Spellbound.

Wayne Stone made a loud sound at the back of his throat. "We've taken the opportunity to review the information provided by the coven."

"Very resourceful witches in your group," Juliet added. "We're quite impressed." She shot a heated look in Lorenzo's direction. "Some of us are, anyway."

Lord Lewis Gilder regarded me. "Pretend this is a case you're about to take before a judge. If we decide to elect you to perform the summoning, what are the odds of success?"

I paused thoughtfully. "Honestly, I have no clue, Lord Gilder. This isn't something I've ever done before. All I can tell you is that I will do everything in my power to get that horn. I want to break the curse as much as anyone."

"You realize that even if you manage to summon the unicorn and retrieve the horn," Lady Weatherby said, "it does not guarantee that the curse will be broken."

"I know," I said, "but it will bring us one step closer." One Yeti-sized step.

"And you will prepare her well for eventualities?" Lord Gilder addressed the head of the coven.

Eventualities? A lump formed in my throat. What did he mean?

"The coven will prepare her to the best of our ability," she replied. "You've reviewed the parchment the same as me, Lewis. It isn't entirely clear what to expect. Know, however, that we are committed to Miss Hart's safety as well as her success."

Lorenzo fixated on me. "You should know that the council will not provide you with any assistance should the summoning go awry. We will not risk the lives of others should you prove unable to carry your weight."

"Carry her weight?" Maeve McCullen echoed. "She's trying to help us break the bloody curse. We should be on our knees thanking her for her sacrifice."

I gulped. Sacrifice? Eventualities? Suddenly my participation felt like a poorly conceived idea.

Maeve tossed her strawberry blond ringlets over her

shoulder. "I still think we should offer whatever help she may need. It's for the benefit of everyone, after all."

"The matter has been fully debated and a decision reached," Lorenzo said, a low growl creeping into his voice.

"Only because of your intimidation tactics," the banshee muttered.

"I'm happy to proceed without help," I said. "I wouldn't be able to forgive myself if anything happened to an innocent paranormal because of my mistake."

"This is exactly the reason why she'll succeed in getting the horn," Juliet said. "I can't see many werewolves showing such an acute sense of guilt and empathy."

"Those emotions are overrated," Lorenzo grumbled.

"Let's not use this as an opportunity to tear each other down," Lucy said. "We're here to build Emma up."

"Indeed," Lord Gilder agreed. "She requires our moral support, if nothing else."

"Thank you," I said.

Wayne glanced down the length of the table. "I guess we should make it official. Upon review of the matter, we've decided to allow Miss Emma Hart to summon the sacred unicorn and retrieve its horn on behalf of Spellbound."

I clutched my stomach, hoping to keep the contents where they belonged through sheer force of will.

"The summoning shall commence one week from today," Lord Gilder announced. "We wish you the best of luck."

I rose to my feet. "Thank you for your approval. I'll do my best not to let you down." I shifted my attention to Lorenzo. "Not a single one of you."

The werewolf only scowled.

I left the Great Hall with Lady Weatherby, who insisted that we go straight to Mix-n-Match to start collecting the ingredients for the summoning identified by Laurel.

"Gathering the ingredients and performing the spell will be the easy part," she said, as I hurried to keep pace with her long strides. "It's what comes after that will be the true test."

I followed her around the shop, hunting for the crucial items. Jemima trailed behind us, effortlessly nosy. With news of the summoning about to become public knowledge, Lady Weatherby wasted no time telling Jemima our reasons for being there.

"What if she gets the spell wrong?" Jemima asked. "What will happen to her?" She sounded downright giddy at the prospect of something going wrong.

Lady Weatherby looked down her nose at Jemima. "And why would she get the spell wrong?"

"She's a remedial witch..." Jemima began to say, but then seemed to think better of it.

"She's a sorceress training privately with me," Lady Weatherby said. "Are you questioning my ability to prepare Miss Hart?"

"No, of course not," Jemima said quickly. "I was just wondering..."

"Negative thoughts such as yours do not help our cause," Lady Weatherby said. "I advise you to keep them to yourself. Miss Hart has enough pressure without feeling like her own coven believes that she'll fail."

"I wasn't suggesting that," Jemima said.

"Good," Lady Weatherby said. "Now run along to the stockroom and fetch me lizard bile."

"You need it for the summoning spell?" she asked.

"No," Lady Weatherby said. "I just want you to spend time in the stockroom with lizard bile and learn to think before you speak."

Jemima bowed her head and hustled off to the stockroom.

I glanced at Lady Weatherby, desperate not to smile. "You don't think you were a little hard on her?"

Lady Weatherby kept her attention on the colored bottles on the shelf in front of us. "Are you questioning me now as well?"

"No, ma'am," I said, straightening. "Wouldn't dream of it."

"Here," Lady Weatherby said, pulling a yellow bottle from the shelf. "You'll need to make a paste with this. And this." She retrieved a green tonic from the shelf below. "I'll show you how."

"This all seems very complicated."

"You're an intelligent young witch." She sighed. "I mean, sorceress. You'll figure it out with practice."

"Were you surprised the council supported the coven's decision?" I asked.

"No, nor was I surprised that they declined to offer official help." Lady Weatherby examined a small vial before placing it back on the shelf. "Lorenzo Mancini truly dislikes you. Whatever did you do to offend him?"

"Nothing," I said. "Okay, maybe he thinks I accused him of crimes here and there. I guess I can understand his displeasure. Anyway, he's not the only one who dislikes me. Someone poisoned my plant recently. Althea is fit to be tied."

Lady Weatherby's head snapped toward me. "Poisoned your plant? In your house?"

"My office," I said. "Don't worry. I've put a protective spell on the doors and windows now. My house was already warded."

"And why would someone poison your plant?"

"I don't know. To send a message?" I had to admit, it was better than a horse head in my bed.

"Do you think someone intends you harm?" Lady Weatherby sounded genuinely concerned.

"I hope not or they'll have to answer to Althea." The Gorgon was not happy with the dead plant or the threat to my well-being.

"We cannot have you at risk at such a critical time," Lady Weatherby said. "Please keep me informed should anything else occur in this vein."

"Yes, ma'am." I stood in silence, watching her carefully select the remainder of the items. "Are you worried?"

"Worried?" She turned to look at me. "About what?"

"About me screwing this up," I said. "If this is our big chance, are you worried that I'm not the right person for the job?" I was, after all, the one who recently knocked her unconscious with a tranquilizer dart.

"I do not have the luxury of worry," Lady Weatherby said. "We simply need to get on with it."

"You would've done well during the Blitz," I said. "You have the stiffest upper lip of anyone in Spellbound."

Lady Weatherby returned her attention to the shelf. "I shall take that as a compliment."

"It is."

"As long as you offer us your very best effort, I will be satisfied."

"But what if I blow our only chance?" I asked.

Her expression darkened. "As I told Jemima, there is no room for negativity. We must prepare well and hope that luck meets opportunity."

There was one question I still wanted to ask. "If there weren't these purity requirements...If you could choose anyone in town to do the summoning, who would it be?"

A brief moment passed before Lady Weatherby turned again to face me. "I'm still looking at her, Miss Hart."

CHAPTER 13

I SPENT the majority of the evening entwined with Daniel on the sofa, updating him on the summoning and the council's decision.

"If anything goes wrong, that Lorenzo Mancini will have to answer to me," Daniel said.

"Nothing will go wrong." Hopefully, I managed to disguise the fear in my voice.

He hugged me tightly. "I'd get the horn myself if I could, but we all know I couldn't pass the purity requirements."

"About that..." I began. "You know what that means for us, right? In light of our recent conversation..."

Daniel stroked my hair. "I told you before. I'll wait an eternity for you, Emma. A little longer is but a drop in the ocean."

I plucked the fabric on the cushion, remembering my conversation with Dr. Hall. "I think before we take that next step, I would like some sign of commitment from you."

His brow lifted. "A sign? Like marriage?"

"It doesn't need to be marriage," I said. "I know you said

126

you were, but it would be nice to have more than words to show me you're in this for the long haul."

"Don't move in," Gareth interjected. "Please don't let that be the sign."

I shot him a death glare, as useless as that was for the dead undead vampire.

"You know I love you, Emma," he said. "And I'll do whatever you want to prove that I'm with you now and always." He kissed me so tenderly that I melted against him.

"Okay, I'm not asking for a sign this minute. I just wanted to let you know my thoughts." As much as I wanted to snuggle a little longer, I made a move to drag myself off the sofa.

"Whoa, hang on a second," he said, pulling back toward him. "I was all nice and cozy, talking about the future. Where are you going?"

"I promised Astrid I'd go to harp therapy with Britta tonight. Britta hasn't been going because she had a falling out with someone, so she hasn't been sleeping well again. Astrid's worried about her."

"With everything you just told me, don't you think you have enough on your plate?" he asked.

"It's only an hour and Britta needs help."

Daniel sighed. "I love your generous spirit, but sometimes it's almost too generous."

"Now you sound like Millie," I said. "She called me a self-appointed humanitarian. If I can fit it into my schedule, then why not?"

"For once, I agree with the Winged Wonder," Gareth said. "You tend to take on too much. Have Astrid go to harp therapy with her sister."

"Astrid's never been," I said to Gareth. "Britta will feel more comfortable if I go because I'm somewhat of a regular."

"See?" Daniel said. "It sounds like Gareth agrees with me."

"You two can feel righteous together after I leave." I heard the beep of a horn outside. "There's Britta now. Goodnight to both of you. Daniel, I'll see you tomorrow." I stood on my tiptoes and gave him a quick kiss.

I didn't wait for any further objections. I grabbed a cardigan from the bottom of the staircase and sailed out the door.

Ten minutes later Britta and I stood outside the church, preparing to go inside.

"Are you ready?" I asked.

"Yes," Britta said, with more confidence than I expected. The Valkyrie took a powerful step forward and then stopped, as though grabbed by an invisible hand.

"Are you okay?" I asked.

Britta stared at the church. "I don't know. I think I want to go home. Sleepless nights aren't so bad."

I studied her closely. She was one of the toughest residents of Spellbound. Something was bothering her other than the argument with the unnamed class member.

"Britta," I said. "You're a Valkyrie, not to mention the deputy in the best town in the whole world. Whatever happened, let's go in the church and work this out."

"Can't," she mumbled.

I placed my hands on my hips. "Britta, what was the argument about?"

She began to examine the blades of grass beneath her feet. "Don't remember."

"Then why are you so concerned? I'm sure the other party doesn't remember either." I tugged on her arm, but she refused to budge.

"What if she doesn't like me anymore?" she asked.

"Huh? Who?"

"Paisley. I made such a wereass of myself. What if she doesn't want to talk to me anymore?"

"Paisley is a lovely witch. If you're truly friends, then I'm sure she'll overlook whatever happened," I assured her.

"But what if I don't want to be friends?" Britta said stubbornly.

I gave an exasperated sigh. "If you don't want to be friends, then why do you care about her opinion of you? Just march in there, ignore her, and pluck those harp strings to your heart's desire."

At the mention of 'heart's desire,' Britta's cheeks turned crimson. In the moonlight, the situation became clear. There hadn't been a friendship-ending argument at all. Britta didn't want to be friends because she wanted to be *more* than friends. And she'd somehow embarrassed herself in front of her crush.

"You're worried that if you go in there, Paisley's going to reject you in front of the whole class," I said gently.

"I don't think she likes me that way," Britta said.

I squeezed her arm. "Unfortunately, there's only one way to find out."

Britta's expression was hopeful. "You'll pass her a note and ask her?"

I squinted. "No. This isn't third grade."

"How did you figure out that Daniel liked you the way you liked him?" she asked.

I laughed. "Trust me. That's not an experience you want to emulate. Lots of angst and malicious spells were involved."

Britta tilted her chin up to gaze at the stars. "I don't even know if she swings my way. I tried to stop myself from crushing on her until I knew for sure, but it was too late. If she weren't so likable, it would be easier to ignore it."

I knew that feeling all too well. "Sometimes our feelings can't be helped. It's what we do with them that matters."

Britta dug the toe of her boot in the dirt. "She has to

know the truth. She's too smart not to have picked up on my feelings."

"Maybe she's willfully oblivious," I suggested.

"Because she doesn't want to know?"

"Maybe. Or maybe she knows, but she's scared, too," I said. "Look, the only way to know for certain is to get your Valkyrie butt in there and feel her out."

Britta's eyes popped. "That's, like, not appropriate in a church."

I rolled my eyes. "Feel her out, not up. Get a sense of how she feels about you."

"Oh." She inhaled deeply and thumped her fist twice on her chest. "I'm ready, Hart. Lead on."

"It's harp therapy, not a battle," I said.

She grabbed me by the wrist and pulled me into the church. "Close enough."

We passed Myra, the church administrator, who was sprucing up artificial flowers in a vase.

"Evening, ladies," Myra said with a smirk. The gnome was always on the lookout for juicy gossip and I wondered whether she'd overheard any of our conversation. For Britta's sake, I hoped not.

"Hey there, Myra," I said, giving a polite wave.

"Haven't seen you here for a bit, Emma," Myra said. "Or you either, Britta."

"Been busy," Britta grumbled. "Deputy and all."

"I've been preoccupied, too," I said.

"Sorcery business?" Myra asked. "Or maybe that angel of yours needs your constant attention? Can't say I'd blame you for giving in to that handsome hunk of halo."

Ooh. She was fishing hard. Well, she could bait me all she wanted. She wasn't getting diddly squat.

"Sorry. Top secret coven business," I replied smoothly. "I'd tell you, but Lady Weatherby would have to kill you."

Myra's expression grew pinched. "Enjoy your class." She beat a hasty retreat to her office.

Britta grinned. "I need you as a buffer more often."

"I'm usually not that brazen," I said. "But Myra brings it out in me. She's such a gossip."

We made our way to the basement for class. Sadly, the brownies had already been claimed, but there were several available harps. I caught sight of Paisley in the middle of the room. As luck would have it, there was an empty seat beside her. I nudged Britta forward.

"What about you?" she hissed.

"There's a chair on the other side of Phoebe," I said. "I'll sit there." It was still within earshot of Britta and her crush, so I could intervene if I had to.

"Look who's back, Sheena," Phoebe said.

Sheena leaned over and waved a chubby hand. "Nice to see you, Emma. We were wondering if we'd frightened you away from harp therapy."

"Not possible," Phoebe said. "If she were that easily frightened, she would've thrown herself off Curse Cliff when she first laid eyes on that furry, one-eyed monster in her house."

"Magpie isn't a monster," I said. *Most of the time.*

"Or when she was attacked by a goblin," Melvin said. "That would have frightened me off, for sure."

"A chip in your teacup would've frightened you off," Phoebe shot back.

"I've been busy," I said. "That's all. I'm sorry I haven't been around as much."

"A likely story," Sheena said.

"Or how about when that vampire ghost roommate of hers made his first appearance?" Phoebe said, reveling in my frightening Spellbound experiences. She seemed to be on a roll. "She wasn't scared off by that either. "

I smiled. "He had leather pants in the closet and a disco ball above his coffin. How could I be frightened of Gareth?"

"Just out of curiosity, where are the leather pants now?" Melvin asked.

"Who are you kidding? They wouldn't fit your faun legs," Phoebe snapped.

As everyone bickered around me, I tried to keep a subtle eye on Britta and Paisley. I had no idea whether Paisley had a romantic interest in the deputy. If not, I didn't want Britta to be traumatized by one negative experience. It couldn't be easy for her. I knew how difficult Gareth had found living in a small town with a hidden identity. At least Britta seemed willing to embrace her true self at a younger age. As old as the vampire was, Gareth still waited until death to come out of the coffin. Now it was too late.

"Are those two doing the naked tango?" Phoebe whispered, noticing the object of my attention. I guess I wasn't as subtle as I thought.

"Clearly not," I replied. "They're fully clothed and engaged in polite conversation. You really should consider getting your eyes checked."

"So I can see these ugly faces more clearly?" Phoebe scoffed. "Not a chance."

Britta appeared in good spirits as she plucked the strings and continued her conversation with Paisley. Whatever embarrassment had passed between them during a previous class seemed to have been forgotten.

I let the chatter fade into the background as I focused on the music. The sound was as calming as I remembered. With all the stress of the murder and the summoning, I didn't realize how badly I needed this until now. Sitting in the chair plucking away at the melodic strings, I was glad I'd decided to join Britta. Being here reminded me that this class was a soothing sanctuary, with or without amazing brownies. The whole reason I'd started to come in the first place was to release tension. What did Daniel and Gareth know? Maybe if they spent more time helping others, they'd end up with more instances of personal satisfaction, too.

"What are you smiling about, witch?" Phoebe asked.

"Don't forget," Melvin said. "She's a sorceress now. She's leveled up."

Phoebe snorted. "If by leveling up, you mean she gets to throw glitter around with her hands instead of using a wand, then I guess she has."

"She's not a fairy," Sheena chided her.

Phoebe gave me the once-over. "No, she's too smart and her boobs aren't big enough."

"There are plenty of spells to change that," Sheena said. "You should talk to some of your coven sisters, Emma."

"I'm happy the way I am, thanks," I replied.

I glanced at Britta, who gave me a not-so-subtle thumbs up. Glad things were going well over there.

"Ooh, look," Melvin exclaimed, shifting his bottom. "I was sitting on half a brownie." He held the crumbling chunk out to me. "Here, Emma. You haven't had any for a while. You should have it."

"I couldn't possibly take that from you, Melvin. You go ahead and enjoy it."

He took a bite of the delicious brownie. "Your loss. I hope you start showing up here again. Class hasn't been the same without you."

"Don't make her head any bigger than it already is," Phoebe said. "It's exactly the same, just one less paranormal to mock." She cocked her head like the bird woman she was. "But let's be clear—you are one of my favorites to make fun of."

I sank into the chair, my smile widening. I had to admit, it was nice to be missed.

CHAPTER 14

"Is that what you're going to wear?" Gareth asked, scrutinizing me.

Daniel and I had been invited to a party thrown by Markos to celebrate the opening of his new venue. At first I'd objected to taking time away from preparation for the summoning, but both Gareth and Daniel insisted that I needed a break from the pressure. It didn't take long for me to fold. As the day drew closer, I grew increasingly anxious and that was the last thing anyone wanted.

I faced Gareth, hands on hips. "I know you're asking that question because you've decided that I made the perfect choice for tonight and you simply can't believe it."

He held up a ghostly finger. "Close, but no. That dress looks like Cinderella's *after* her naughty stepsisters tore it to shreds."

I glanced down at my outfit. It wasn't *that* bad, was it? I turned to Sedgwick. "What do you think?"

The owl blinked his large yellow eyes. *I'm an owl. I don't do fashion.*

I threw up my hands. "Great. Sedgwick doesn't like it either."

"You should have let Daniel buy something new for you," Gareth said. "If nothing else, the angel has excellent taste."

Not to mention years of experience buying dresses for women, Sedgwick added.

I narrowed my eyes at my familiar. "Keep it up and I'll make sure you're tied to my leg during the summoning. If anything goes south, I'll sacrifice you like a mother kangaroo with a spare joey."

Sedgwick studied me closely. *You wouldn't dare.*

I shrugged nonchalantly. "I might. I would think it's customary for a familiar to accompany his companion into the bowels of hell. Show solidarity."

Gareth chuckled. "Are you threatening the poor owl?"

"Not a threat," I said. "Just an idea."

Here's an idea, Sedgwick said. *Change your dress.*

"Okay, fine." I pulled the dress up and over my head and returned to the closet for another option.

"This is a Markos party," Gareth reminded me. "You want to look like you care."

"I *do* care," I said. "Markos is one of the sweetest paranormals in town and I want to show my support."

"He's not sweet," Gareth said. "He's in love, but that's another story."

"He is not in love," I objected. "He's a soft-hearted minotaur. That's all. Too bad he's not a virgin or he'd be an ideal candidate for the summoning."

"He's not a magic user," Gareth said.

"It's not too late to teach him how to do the spell," I said. "Come to think of it, maybe we should send him instead."

"Don't get cold feet," Gareth said, lifting a deep purple dress from the recess of the closet. "This is the perfect color for your hair and skin tone."

I touched the crepe fabric. "I like this dress. I keep forgetting it's in there."

"That's because you let Lucy take you shopping too often," Gareth said. "The fairy has an addiction."

"She's calmed down since becoming mayor," I said. "She's too busy to shop."

"All the better for you," Gareth replied. He removed the hanger and handed the dress to me.

Magpie appeared on the bed seemingly from nowhere.

"Great," I said. "An audience." I slipped the dress over my head and adjusted the neckline.

"Ah. That's the one." Gareth inclined his head, admiring the results.

"You're just saying that because you chose it and you don't want to be wrong."

"Aye, maybe so," he replied. "But take a look in that wee mirror and judge for yourself."

I stood in front of the full-length mirror and twirled. He was right, as usual. The dress was perfect.

"You win," I said. "Where's my handbag?"

"Your handbag?" Gareth queried.

I blinked. "Yes. Daniel will be here any minute. It's time to go."

Gareth's fang bit into his lip. "But…"

"What is it, Gareth?"

He peered at my head. "Is that how you're going to wear your hair?"

The Tiki Bar was cooler than any place I'd been in Spellbound. It was an outdoor bar with one of his famous mazes attached—a genius move for the inebriated crowd. No one would ever leave because they wouldn't be able to find their way out. Fey lanterns designed to look like Tiki torches

A DROP IN THE POTION

dotted the perimeter and the bar had a South Pacific vibe. The maze was adjacent to the bar area and was also illuminated by faux Tiki torches. A band played on a platform beside the bar and I recognized Nameless Faces. They really were the hot new band in town.

"Markos has really upped his game," I said, surveying the scene. "This place is incredible."

Daniel squeezed my waist. "Some paranormals claim he was inspired by a muse."

I glanced up at him. "Are you implying I inspired this place?" I laughed. "That's nuts. There's nothing about this that says Emma Hart. Markos is a genius with a minotaur head full of ideas."

"A genius, huh?" Daniel smiled. "Should I be jealous?"

"Not in a million years," I said, and stood on my tiptoes to kiss his cheek. He leaned down to accommodate my eager lips.

The minotaur of the hour appeared in front of us. "Spellbound's favorite couple," Markos said. "I'm so glad you're here."

I gave Markos a fierce hug. No easy feat when he was in his minotaur form. I couldn't even wrap my arms all the way around him.

"You look beautiful," he whispered.

"Thank you." I pulled back to get a better view of him. "Did you polish your horns? They're so shiny tonight."

He touched the tip of his horn. "I did. Thank you for noticing."

"She notices everything," Daniel said. "It's both a blessing and a curse."

"Not everything," a voice said. Beatrice moved to stand beside Markos. I'd been wary of the witch ever since I'd had a bad experience in my therapist's office. I'd had a waking nightmare thanks to a spell gone wrong, and I was fairly

137

certain Beatrice had done it to me on purpose because she was jealous of my relationship with Markos. I didn't want another Elsa Knightsbridge on my hands, especially when I had no romantic interest in Markos.

"You know my office manager, Beatrice," Markos said.

I forced a smile. "I do."

"How's the dreamscaping going?" Beatrice asked.

My expression soured. "That's confidential information," I said. What took place in my therapist's office really shouldn't be making the rounds at a party. Dr. Hall would have a fit if she knew.

Beatrice covered her mouth in a half-hearted attempt to silence herself. "Oops, sorry. I assumed your boyfriend knew."

I slid an arm around Daniel's waist. "He does know, but that doesn't make it appropriate party conversation."

"An innocent mistake, right?" Markos looked at Beatrice, awaiting her nod of agreement.

"Of course. I would never dare do anything to upset Spellbound's unofficial princess." She smiled and sipped her cocktail, like she'd made a joke.

"You mean official sorceress," Daniel said, attempting to smooth over the awkward exchange.

"I'm surprised you're here," Beatrice said. "I told Markos you'd be far too busy preparing for the summoning to turn up at a party."

"Daniel and I decided it would be a good distraction for me. Get out of the house and get out of my head," I said. "I tend to stress out more when I'm home. I think too much and the anxiety takes over."

"And yet you're the one they chose to perform the summoning." Beatrice clucked her tongue. "Sometimes you have to wonder what the coven is brewing."

"Emma will make us proud," Daniel said. He gazed at me

with such adoration, the rest of the world faded away. "She's been preparing with Lady Weatherby and has the full support of the council."

"Not *everyone*," Beatrice said. "I heard Lorenzo Mancini was against it."

Markos gave an embarrassed laugh. "Beatrice, Emma is my guest, not to mention a good friend. Let's show our support."

Her eyes widened with false innocence. "I'm so sorry. I thought that's what I was doing. Was it misinterpreted?"

"That's okay," Markos said. "I know you didn't mean anything by it."

Yikes, she sure had him fooled.

"Have you seen the maze yet?" Markos asked, changing the topic of conversation. "I think it's my best work yet."

"On our way now," I said, ready to put as much distance between Beatrice and us as possible.

Markos stepped forward, ready to escort us, but Beatrice grabbed his elbow.

"Markos, I think your guests need livelier music," she said. "Maybe have a word with the band."

Markos shifted his gaze from me to the band. "You think so? Everyone seems to be enjoying it."

"They sound great," I enthused. Hearing them for a second time, I could understand what all the fuss was about.

"Thank you," Markos said. "Enjoy the maze and best of luck with the summoning. You know we're all rooting for you."

Not all of them, judging by the look in Beatrice's eyes.

"Well, that wasn't at all awkward," Daniel whispered as we headed toward the maze.

"What?"

"Don't feign innocence," he said. "She clearly doesn't like you. Is it because of the minotaur?"

"Don't call him the minotaur," I said. "His name is Markos and he's our host tonight."

"I don't object to being called 'the angel,'" Daniel said.

"That's different," I said.

Daniel cocked his head. "Why?"

"Because when you say 'the minotaur,' it sounds derogatory," I said. "Nobody says 'the angel' in a derogatory way."

"No, but they say 'fallen angel' or 'womanizing angel' or 'Halo Boy.'"

I smiled at the last one. "I do have a soft spot for Cloud Hopper and Winged Wonder."

He pulled me closer. "Do you now? And what am I to call you? Sorcery seductress? Bewitching witch?"

I tilted my chin up to gaze into his turquoise eyes. "Emma."

"That'll do," he replied. His lips met mine and my legs did that thing they always seemed to do when Daniel kissed me —they turned to jelly.

"Get a room," a voice cracked.

I didn't need to look to recognize the throaty sound of Phoebe Minor. "I didn't expect to see you here, Phoebe."

"Free booze and hot men," she replied. "Why would I be anywhere else? I'm surprised you left the house for anything other than Operation Unicorn."

"It's an attempt to calm my nerves and enjoy myself," I replied.

"You two seem to be doing just fine with enjoying yourselves. Maybe you could consider enjoying yourselves in the privacy of your own home. You have two of them between you, after all."

"You're very hung up on men and their own houses." I continued to hug Daniel. "I bet if you really put your mind to it, you could make it happen. I think deep down you like living with your family."

Phoebe gave me an amused look. "Oh? I suppose all that therapy makes you an expert now, huh?"

"Have you tried speed dating? I know of several success stories that came from it, like Karen Duckworth, the librarian."

"And I know of a success story that came from someone who nearly drowned in Swan Lake," Phoebe interjected. "Shall I go and throw myself off the dock to see if my true love swoops down to rescue me?"

I sighed. I'd never win against a harpy with Phoebe's resolve. "Are you the only Minor in attendance this evening?"

"Nope. My nieces are here, mingling." She gesticulated to an adjacent room. "Darcy's dressed like she's ready to run for higher office. She seems to confuse a party with a political party."

"I'll keep an eye out for them," I said, biting back a smile. Darcy was undeniably the uptight harpy in the family. Then again, she volunteered on so many committees in Spellbound, it seemed unfair to say a negative word about her. Very few residents were willing to give their time the way Darcy did. On the other hand, if I lived with a bunch of harpies like Octavia and Phoebe, I'd probably use any excuse to spend time out of the house as well.

Phoebe sniffed the air. "Ooh, I smell an incubus. Best grab him before someone else does." She barely glanced back at me before shuffling toward the buffet table. "Good luck with the summoning, Hart."

"Thank you," I called after her.

We toured the maze, which was every bit as amazing as Markos promised. It took us an hour to find our way through it, not that we minded. There were plenty of dark corners for stolen kisses. Daniel had to tuck his wings in as tightly as they would go. For all the paranormals in town, the maze wasn't designed for the larger-winged kind.

"Are you ready for a drink?" Daniel asked, as we returned to the bar area.

"Yes, and then a dance, please," I said. Any excuse to be in his arms. "Oh, look! I see Begonia and Dem on the dance floor."

Daniel tried his best to hide his disappointment. "There's no avoiding that vampire, is there?"

As we started to make our way to the bar, a familiar figure across the room stopped me. I couldn't believe it. It was Marcie, the gorgeous succubus, and she wasn't far from where Begonia and Demetrius were dancing. What would happen when she saw them together? Did she know about Begonia?

"What's wrong?" Daniel asked, noticing my stiff pose.

I inclined my head toward Marcie. "That's the woman I saw with Demetrius at night."

Daniel glanced her way. "I guess I can see your concern."

"Right? I mean, I know Begonia is young and inexperienced, but that doesn't mean Demetrius should look elsewhere for his needs. Not if he's serious about her."

"Don't assume anything," he said. "You know better than that. To everyone else in town, I'm a fallen angel with a spotty record, but you never saw me that way."

I leaned my head against his arm. "Of course not. That's not the Daniel I know and love. To be fair, I never viewed Demetrius as a womanizing vampire either. He's been nothing but a gentleman with me. Then again, I never really got involved with him romantically."

Daniel slung an arm across my shoulders. "Good thing, too. That vampire already rubbed me the wrong way. Winning you over would've been the last straw."

I tracked Marcie as she wove her way through the dancing bodies. Her gaze landed on Demetrius and she started to head straight for him. I had to stop her. I didn't want Begonia to suffer any public humiliation.

"I need a spell," I said to Daniel. "I need to stop her from talking to Demetrius."

"You worry too much," Daniel replied.

His words barely registered. My attention was fixed on my friend. Begonia looked beautifully blissful cradled in her boyfriend's arms. I didn't want anything to tarnish this moment for her. My sole focus was to protect her from the kind of pain I felt when I saw Daniel and Elsa together. I had to move fast because Marcie was nearly upon them.

Without pausing to decide on a spell, I simply threw out my hands. Not smart. Light exploded. Guests screamed and covered their eyes. Servers dropped their trays, momentarily blinded. I heard the crash of glasses and plates all around me.

"Stars and stones," I whispered.

The bright light quickly faded and everyone looked around, uncertain what happened. No one seemed to suspect me.

"I think one of the fey lanterns burst," I heard someone say.

Daniel stared at the mess I'd created. "I'm guessing that's not what you intended to do."

"Not at all," I said glumly. "I let my emotions control my actions. I should know better than that."

"Can you help clean up the mess?" Daniel asked.

"Yes, but I can't do a anything about that mess." I gestured to the spot where Marcie was now engaged in conversation with Demetrius. Begonia stood by his side, completely oblivious.

I retrieved my wand and concentrated, determined to be more careful this time. "No more, no less/clean up my mess."

Broken glass and plates reformed. Spilled drinks disappeared from the floor and guests' clothing. Everything seemed to be in order.

I covered my face with my hands. "I don't know how I'm going to get this unicorn horn when I can't even keep Begonia from meeting her boyfriend's mistress."

At that moment, Demetrius's gaze met mine and I knew he'd heard me. Stupid vampire hearing! He crossed the room with Begonia in tow.

"Did you say 'mistress'?" Demetrius asked.

I suddenly bore a strong resemblance to a deer in the headlights. "Mistress? No, of course not. I said seamstress. She hems your trousers, right?"

Daniel grinned at me. "You know you're not British, right? We say pants here."

"Gareth must be rubbing off on me," I mumbled.

Demetrius appeared stunned. "You definitely said mistress. Do you think Marcie and I are having a thing?"

"Maybe," I said, beginning to feel embarrassed. "Look at her. She's gorgeous." I squeezed Begonia's arm. "Not that you aren't." Begonia was beautiful inside and out. That was one of the reasons I adored her.

"I told you Marcie is an old friend," Demetrius said.

"Isn't 'old friend' code for 'new side piece'?" I asked.

Hurt flashed in the vampire's eyes. "Marcie also happens to be a realtor."

Begonia glanced at him. "You're moving?" Not that moving was a concern in Spellbound. He couldn't go very far.

Demetrius sighed. "I wanted it to be a surprise, but I can see I'd better tell you the truth."

"The truth?" Begonia queried.

I clenched my fists, ready for his confession.

"Marcie has been showing me empty office spaces."

Begonia scrunched her nose. "What do you need an office for?"

He took her hand. "I don't need an office, but you do. For your business, Spelled Ink. You've been so busy with school, but I know you really want to get this tattoo shop off the ground. I thought if I did the legwork checking out spaces available for lease, that it would help you get started."

Begonia's eyes brimmed with tears. "I can't believe you've been spending your free time looking at rental spaces for me. No one's ever done anything like that for me before."

I was horrified by my mistake. Right now I needed a spell that would allow the floor to swallow me whole.

"I'm so sorry, Dem. I feel awful. I shouldn't have doubted you." I generally considered myself an open-minded and supportive person, yet I had doubted Demetrius at the first opportunity. Once again, I questioned whether I was the right choice for the summoning. Ugh. I should never have left the house tonight.

He shook his dark head. "Water under a troll's bridge, Emma. I know your heart was in the right place. It always is."

Begonia wanted to hear more about the property search. "So have you found anything good?"

"I've narrowed it down to three," Demetrius said. "Obviously, it makes sense for you to make the final decision. Marcie's been a huge help."

"But I can't afford a lease until I start to make money," Begonia said.

Demetrius grinned. "Consider me your vampire investor. Our money is every bit as good as the angels'."

Begonia could barely contain her excitement. "This is amazing! I can't possibly thank you enough. When can we see the spaces? Can we go now?"

Demetrius chuckled. "Why don't we enjoy the rest of the

party tonight? I'm sure Marcie will be more than happy to take us for viewings tomorrow."

Begonia threw her arms around him and kissed him firmly on the lips. "You're the best boyfriend ever. Has anyone ever told you that?"

Dem's expression turned serious. "To be honest, you'd be the first."

I snuck a peek at Daniel and saw the same thought reflected in his eyes—that maybe he and Demetrius weren't so different after all.

CHAPTER 15

THE DAY of the summoning was almost here and there was one more source I decided to visit in preparation for the big day. Although I'd seen Lyra recently at my house where she worked on Gareth's poltergeist skills, I hadn't seen her sisters. The Grey sisters were unlike any of the other paranormals in town and seemed to have their bony fingers on the pulse of more than just Spellbound. If anyone had advice to offer about the summoning, it was the ancient sisters.

I stood outside the cave on the outskirts of town with a headless chicken in a bag, and used my wand to ring an imaginary bell. Okay, so it wasn't earth-shattering magic, but it was a bit of fun and I enjoyed it.

"A visitor, we have," Effie, the taller sister said, coming to greet me at the mouth of the cave. She wore the single eye she shared with the shorter sister. Thanks to me, Lyra had her own eyes and a full set of chompers.

"Hello, Effie," I said. "Is this a bad time?"

She lifted a white and grey eyebrow. "A chicken, you have?"

I held up the bag for inspection.

"Not a bad time to see you at all," she replied. "Come, come. My sisters will be pleased, they will."

I followed her into the sparse cave to the room where her sisters were seated on stone chairs with a loom between them. Petra, the shorter sister, sat with a ball of yarn in her lap.

"Oh no," I said. "This isn't the thing where you decide it's time for someone to die, is it?" I glanced around the cave for a pair of scissors.

"Not the Fates are we," Petra snapped.

"Sorry," I said quickly. "It wasn't meant as an insult."

"No control over fate do we have," Lyra said, rising to her feet. "We would not be here otherwise."

They may lack control, but it didn't mean they lacked knowledge.

"Have you heard about the summoning?" I asked.

The trio nodded in sync.

"Hear much, but say little," Effie said. "A pivotal moment yet to come."

"That's why I'm here," I said. "I don't want to mess it up. I'm hoping you have advice for me. I'm terrified I won't get the horn." Or worse.

Lyra made a noise at the back of her throat. "Sacred unicorns are like a total eclipse. Rare and wonderful."

"There seems to be a distinction between sacred unicorns and regular unicorns." The idea of a garden-variety unicorn made me want to laugh. "What's the difference?"

"Blessed with the golden horn the sacred unicorn is," Petra said. "Other unicorns wear a horn of white."

Ah. "So it's a *golden* horn I need for the spell to break the curse."

"Golden, yes," Lyra replied. "Like the sun."

"Like a halo," Effie added.

The mention of a halo immediately conjured an image of

Daniel in my mind. "Is there anything I need to know about getting the unicorn to offer up its horn? I mean, I know I need to be...pure in more ways than one."

"Yes, a virgin you must be," Petra said.

A blush crept into my cheeks. "Yes, we've established that part. Anything else I should know? Advice like don't look a unicorn directly in the eye or don't tell it my name or it will enslave me forever? You know, minor details like that."

"A vivid imagination you have," Lyra said.

"Who needs a vivid imagination when I live in Spellbound?" I said.

Petra set her yarn on top of a pile of cloth and stood. "Treat the beast with respect."

"Of course," I said. How could you treat a sacred unicorn with anything *but* respect?

"Start at the beginning," Effie added.

"Where's the beginning?" I asked. The parchment didn't say *where* to perform the summoning. In the end, the council decided to choose a convenient spot on the outskirts of town where no innocent bystanders would be caught in the crosshairs.

"The place where you start," Petra replied.

Sometimes those Grey sisters were infuriating. See if I bring them a headless chicken next time!

"Do not let fear guide your actions," Lyra warned.

"Everyone says that the unicorn won't hurt me," I said. "What else is there to be afraid of?"

The three Grey sisters began to circle me.

"Not so simple as requesting its horn," Lyra said. "Challenges lie ahead."

"Yes, Raisa said there would be obstacles," I said. "Do you know what kind of challenges to expect?" They were making me dizzy, walking around me in a clockwise pattern.

"You must prove your worth," Effie said.

"Yes, I know. Pure of heart, mind, and body. Got it."

Petra snatched the eye from her sister to stare at me. "Overcome the obstacles and that shall be proof."

"Are you sure the unicorn won't just take my word for it?" I asked, only partially joking. "I can offer a signed affidavit. Emma Hart is the purest pure girl in Puretown. Stan can even notarize it."

No one laughed.

"Very little she knows," Petra said from behind me.

I spun around to address her. "Then tell me everything I need to know. It's for your benefit as much as mine. Don't you want to break the curse?"

They stopped walking and fell silent.

"Do not let fear guide your actions." Lyra repeated her earlier warning.

I could tell this was as much information as I was likely to get. "Thank you for your help."

Effie placed her long fingers on my shoulder, her nails gently scraping my exposed skin. "Take care, Emma Hart," the tall sister said. "The task is no simple one."

"It seems only right that you serve as my fashion coordinator for the big day." I watched as Gareth selected my summoning outfit and placed it on the bed.

"It's my contribution to the cause," he said.

I touched the comfortable fabric of the pants. Light and fluid. Perfect for running...from what I didn't want to know.

"I know we're not breaking any curses today," I said, "but are you concerned about that at all?"

Gareth busied himself selecting an understated pair of earrings from the jewelry box. Nothing too showy.

"Why would I be concerned about breaking the curse?" he queried.

I sat on the bed. "The whole reason you're here with me is because they wouldn't admit you to the next life." Whatever that is for vampires. "The curse kept you in Spellbound, even as a ghost. If the curse breaks..." I trailed off, unable to finish the thought.

Gareth floated beside me and handed me a pair of simple pearl earrings. "One step at a time now, lass. There's plenty of opportunity to fret *after* you bring back the horn."

Magpie jumped onto the bed, causing the outfit to wrinkle. Gareth's fangs popped out and Magpie scampered to the pillow, curling into an apologetic ball.

A wave of emotion washed over me. "I don't ever want to lose you," I said.

Gareth's expression softened. "Did you take your anti-anxiety potion this morning?"

I held up two fingers. "A double dose. Boyd's suggestion."

"He's a wise druid," Gareth said. "The best healer this town has."

"I dreamed last night that the unicorn turned out to be a Pegasus." I shuddered. "I really don't want to fly."

"You'll do whatever is necessary to get that horn," Gareth said. "Because that's who you are."

"Let's get this over and done with," I said, securing the earrings to my lobes. "I need to get back to my normal life." I paused. "Okay, my not-so-normal life, but still. There's a murder to solve."

"I thought you said you had your eye on Franklin Sutcliffe," Gareth said.

"Astrid has been tailing him, but she hasn't noticed anything out of the ordinary. He's also continuing to hang around Jemima at Mix-n-Match, which suggests his presence there might be genuine."

I felt a light pressure as Gareth kissed me on the cheek.

"Not to worry," he said. "Like I told you before, one step at a time."

Once I was fully dressed and wrapped in a coven cloak, I went downstairs where Daniel awaited me.

"Breakfast is on the table," he said. "I'd love to take credit, but Gareth beat me to it."

I shrugged. "He loves to cook."

"And it's *my* house," Gareth called from upstairs.

I ignored my roommate and joined Daniel in the dining room where a healthy bowl of porridge sat on the table.

"I wanted to cook eggs, but Gareth insisted porridge was better for a day full of...activity."

I mixed a spoonful of honey into the porridge and stirred. "Thank you both for being so supportive."

"Are you sure you don't want me to fly you to the starting point?" he asked.

After discussing the Grey sisters' recommendation to 'start at the beginning' with Gareth and Daniel, we decided I would go to Curse Cliff. At first I thought they meant Swan Lake—my beginning in Spellbound—but Curse Cliff made more sense since that was where the curse on the town was initiated.

I shook my head. "I need to start this day on the ground because I have no idea what to expect later. I'm driving to the secret lair first to pick up the ingredients since it's on the way." I thought it was safer to store them in the secret lair than the house.

I finished my porridge and washed it down with a nice cup of tea. It would've been a lovely start to the day if today's events weren't so nerve-racking. I set down my cup and noticed Daniel staring at me.

"What?" I wiped my face. "Do I have porridge on my nose or something?"

"Even if you did, I wouldn't notice," he replied. "You're lit from within. Do you know that?"

"Like a gas oven?"

He reached for my hand. "Make jokes all you like, Emma Hart. I'm still going to love you."

"No matter how bad my jokes are? Because I can up the ante."

The angel tucked a loose strand of hair behind my ear. "I love you. No matter what happens today, carry that close to your heart."

"Always," I whispered.

Sedgwick swooped into the room and perched on the mantel. *It's time, Your Highness.*

I pushed back my chair and tried to steady my ragged breathing. Sensing my fear, Daniel wrapped his arms around me and I shivered with pleasure when his wings tickled my bare skin. I closed my eyes, enjoying the touch of his hands on the small of my back. It was the little things with Daniel that made me happy. Right here and now was the most comfortable place in the world. No matter where we were, the feel of his arms around me told me I was home.

"You'll be amazing today," he said. "I feel it in my bones."

"I hope so," I replied. "Or I'm getting to let down an entire town. Someone already poisoned my plant. Imagine what they'll do to me if I fail."

"Try not to think about it that way," he said, tipping my chin upward. "Think about it as a coven test. Pretend it's one of your law school classes and you desperately want that A plus."

"I never got an A plus. The school didn't offer them."

He pulled back and grinned at me. "Then here's your big chance."

"If something happens to me..."

He kissed my hand. "Nothing is going to happen. You're

coming back to me all in one piece or so help me, I will smite that unicorn myself."

I smiled. "You can smite? I didn't realize you had the power to smite."

"Oh, I can smite with the best of them if the situation requires it."

"Even without your halo?"

"My halo has no effect on my smiting abilities."

I inclined my head. "Have you ever hurt anyone?"

Daniel stroked the back of my hair. "Physically, no. Angels tend to turn the other cheek. But you know the ways in which I've hurt others."

"Is there one instance you regret more than the rest?" I asked.

"Let's keep the focus on positive thoughts," Daniel said. "I don't want you to worry about me and my redemption. I can tell that's what's on your mind right now."

"You know me too well."

When he grinned, my heart skipped a beat. "Jumping off that big rock was the best leap of faith I ever took," he said.

"You're my rock," I said, placing my palms flat on his chest. *Stars and stones, that was one firm chest.* "I'm so lucky to have you."

He leaned down to kiss my forehead. "You're *our* rock, Emma, and we're *all* lucky to have you."

CHAPTER 16

"Are you sure you have the hair of a rat's tongue?" Millie asked, peering over my shoulder at the summoning checklist.

I'd driven to the secret lair and found my friends already there, pacing the floor in anticipation of my arrival. Sedgwick opted to wait outside and the hunt for small lizards.

"For the third time, yes," I said through gritted teeth. "I am flawed in many ways, Millie, but organization is not one of them."

"You're right," she said, backing off. "I'm sorry."

Did my ears deceive me or did Millie just apologize? She was obviously taking the summoning *very* seriously. I took the apology in stride so as not to dissuade her from doing it again someday.

"Why do you have everything lined up like that?" Sophie asked, observing the table.

I pointed to the first item. "It's like a recipe. I lined up each ingredient for the spell in the order in which I intend to use it. It was Gareth's idea."

"Can the spell backfire?" Sophie asked. "What if you accidentally summon something horrible?"

"That's why I'm wearing comfortable shoes," I said. "In case I need to run."

"You should bring your broomstick," Millie said. "In case you need to fly."

"Not a good idea," I said.

Millie fixed me with her hard stare. "Emma, a broomstick can mean the difference between life and death. You should have one with you as a last resort."

"It's not exactly convenient to lug around," I said. "I'd have to strap it to my back like Wonder Woman's sword."

"You at least have your wand, right?" Begonia inquired. "I know your magic manifests differently, but a wand is never a bad idea."

I patted my waistband. "Tiffany is present and accounted for."

"Do you think the whole town will be at Curse Cliff?" Sophie asked.

I shook my head. "The council has warned everyone to stay close to home. They've asked residents to avoid the outskirts of town until tomorrow."

"That's smart," Laurel said. "We don't want anyone interfering."

"How are you feeling?" Begonia asked. "Do you need a hug?"

I held out my arms and she squeezed me tightly. The other girls piled on until we were one huge clump of arms and legs.

"No matter what happens today," I said, "you should all be proud of yourselves. If it weren't for the remedial witches, we wouldn't even have this opportunity right now."

We released our grip on each and I set to work gathering my ingredients and placing them carefully in my satchel.

"Should we walk with you to Curse Cliff?" Laurel asked.

I slung the satchel over my shoulder. "I'd rather you

didn't. Sedgwick will be with me. That's enough company for one summoning."

"Good luck, Emma," Begonia said. "Horn or no horn, we love you."

"Speak for yourself," Millie said. "My love is conditional on achievement."

Laurel frowned. "You sound like your mother, Millie."

Millie's hand flew to cover her mouth. "Stars and stones, I really do."

I waved goodbye and left the secret lair, carrying the dreams of an entire town on my shoulder.

I reached Curse Cliff and kneeled on the ground, emptying the contents of the satchel. I placed seven rocks in a circle and followed the instructions exactly as Lady Weatherby had shown me. I wasn't as adept at mixing ingredients as some of the other witches, but I'd improved with practice. Mostly I disliked touching disgusting items like the hair of a rat's tongue, but when the fate of the town was hanging in the balance, it was easier to focus on the big picture.

I chanted and danced around the perimeter of the rocks until a plume of smoke burst from its center. A blue flame began to burn.

Is that supposed to happen? Sedgwick asked.

"I hope so."

I stopped and waited. Nothing seemed different except for the blue flame.

Any sign yet? Sedgwick asked.

"Not yet. Ask me one more time and I'm going to turn this car around."

You're not in a car.

"Forget it."

I surveyed the landscape, trying to figure out my next

steps. It wasn't long before a flock of white birds appeared in the distance. Instead of forming a V-pattern, they flew in a circle above a section of the forest.

They may as well take the shape of an X, Sedgwick said.

"And we are go for launch."

I left the blue flame burning and trekked across the rocky terrain to the start of the forest. The air immediately felt a good five degrees cooler and I was thankful for the cloak Gareth had insisted I wear. I tried to keep my nerves at bay, choosing to focus on the smiling faces of my friends and loved ones. I pictured how proud my parents and grandparents would be if they could see me now.

"I am brave," I whispered to myself. Maybe if I repeated the mantra enough times, I would start to believe it.

Almost there, Sedgwick informed me. He was in a better position to see the birds since the sky had become obscured by the treetops.

I stopped in my tracks. *Um, Sedgwick. I think we're here.*

In front of a cluster of white birch trees stood two of the Grey sisters, their white and grey hair knotted in braids down their backs.

"What are you doing here?" I asked. "Where's Lyra?"

"We have been called upon to take part in the summoning," Effie replied.

"What about Lyra?" I asked.

"Disallowed," Petra said. Probably because I knew her too well.

I took a careful step backward. "What have you been called upon to do?"

"This phase of the summoning is a test of your mental clarity, it is," Effie said. "Two plants are on the ground before you."

With those words, two plants pushed the dirt aside and emerged from the earth. One plant was green with white berries and the other plant was green with yellow berries. Other than the color of the berries, they appeared identical.

"One of these plants is a deadly poison, it is," Petra said. "The other has magical healing properties."

"And I need to figure out which one is which?" I queried.

"There is more, there is," Petra said. Her grey cloak billowed in the breeze. "Provide information that guides you, we will."

"Except one of us is lying and one of us is telling the truth," Effie said.

"And I have to decide which is which," I said. As the shorter one opened her mouth to speak, I interrupted. "Let me guess. There's more."

Of course there is, Sedgwick said, from his position above me and to the left.

The shorter sister pointed a finger at my familiar and bellowed, "Alight."

I shrieked in horror as orange flames licked Sedgwick's feathers. He plummeted to the ground and rocked in the dirt in an effort to smother the fire.

"Sedgwick!" I ran and dropped to my knees beside him. Although the flames were extinguished, his wings were scorched and he looked close to death.

"We are most sorry," the taller one said with the utmost sincerity.

"Now decide the correct plant more quickly, you must," the shorter one said.

I glared at them over my shoulder. "Like I needed any more pressure." I focused on Sedgwick, stroking his winged feathers. "I'm here for you, buddy. I'll figure out which one is the healing plant."

"Fail and he dies," the taller one said.

I stood and faced them. "Yes, I kinda figured that. So why

159

am I not in pain? He's my familiar. Shouldn't I be feeling the burns?"

"A magical test, this is," the shorter one said. "You are granted a clear head free from pain."

"Not entirely." Even though my body felt fine, my head was muddied with fear for Sedgwick's life. I couldn't screw this up or he would die.

"Ask either one of us a question to help you," Effie said.

I studied the two plants, thinking. This was like a brain teaser. I was good at riddles and brain teasers when I was younger. I could do this. Sedgwick was depending on me.

"Sedgwick, talk to me," I said. "Say something snarky. Anything."

Your butt…looks big from this angle.

Thank goodness. Still alive. "So I ask one of you which is the healing plant, and one of you will lie and one of you will tell me the truth?"

They nodded in unison.

"Are you both telling the truth now?"

They nodded again in unison.

"I guess that didn't count, since you both answered the same way." Okay, time to do this. I needed to give myself a pep talk. "It's a logic puzzle. I may not be able to choose the best outfit, but I *can* do logic puzzles."

"Tick, tick, tick," Effie and Petra said in unison.

I crouched on the ground in front of the plants. I drew an X in the dirt in front of the first plant and a Y in front of the other plant. "There are two possible scenarios. If I ask the sister who lies which plant is the healing plant, she will say…" I paused, thinking. "No. There's a trick." I remembered a game I'd played with my grandfather—something involving knights. "I need to ask one of you what the *other sister* would say if I ask which one is the healing plant."

The Grey sisters remained silent. I glanced over my shoulder at Sedgwick, still motionless on the ground.

"Petra, which plant would Effie say is the healing plant?"

Petra met my steady gaze. "Effie would say the plant marked by an X is the healing plant."

I stared hard at the plants, praying that my understanding of the puzzle was correct. "I choose the plant marked with a Y as the healing plant."

I didn't wait for confirmation. I ripped a piece of the plant from the ground, along with the yellow berries, and rushed to Sedgwick's side. His eyes were closed and his body limp.

"The berries or the leaf?" I asked no one in particular.

"Both," one of the sisters replied. I hoped it was the truth teller.

I squished the berries and broke apart the leaf. A clear liquid dripped onto Sedgwick's feathers. I rubbed the juices over his damaged body until my hands were dry.

"Sedgwick?" I asked hopefully.

His large eyes opened. *How did you know? And please don't say you took a risk when the other plant was a deadly poison.*

"It doesn't matter which sister I ask, I would choose the opposite plant of the one I was told because the result is the same."

How?

"If Petra is the sister who lies, then she will tell me that Effie will point me toward the poison plant. If Petra tells the truth, then she will tell me that Effie, the lying sister, will point me toward the poison plant. Either way, the opposite plant of the one I'm told *must* be the healing plant. Do you see?"

Sedgwick closed his eyes again.

"Sedgwick?" I couldn't keep the panic out of my voice.

I'm fine, he said. *I just have a headache from your explanation.*

"Since you nearly died, I'll forgive your snarky attitude," I said.

He rose from the ground, his wings flapping as though nothing had happened. *Good as new. Let's carry on.*

"No, not you. You need to go home," I said. "I don't want to risk you getting hurt again. I can do this on my own." He was a liability, not because he was incapable, but because I cared about him.

Are you sure? he asked.

I nodded slowly. I didn't trust myself to speak and change my mind.

As you wish, he replied, and flew away.

I watched him go, clamping down on the stirrings of regret, until he was out of sight.

CHAPTER 17

When I turned my attention back to the Grey sisters, they were gone. I took the path that cut between the birch trees and immediately heard the sound of rushing water. I came upon a creek that I'd never seen before. It must feed into Swan Lake. I hadn't even realized it was here.

Gently flapping wings caught my attention and I noticed a beautiful butterfly beside me. Its wings were a brilliant shade of blue with yellow markings. Blue and yellow again, like the pot on my mantel and the wallpaper in my parents' kitchen. Those two colors seemed to be a theme in my life.

"Hey there, pretty fella," I said. "Any chance you can lead me to the unicorn?" It was a long shot, but worth a try.

The butterfly hovered beside me, uncommunicative. I continued to walk alongside the creek, wondering whether I was meant to use it as a guide. The sound of fluttering wings increased and I looked behind me to see that several more butterflies had appeared. They were all the same blue with yellow markings. I didn't recall that butterflies socialized like bees. I had always considered them to be more solitary creatures. They followed behind me and I thought maybe they were curious about my presence here. After another minute of walking, I realized that the sound had become more like a dull vibration. There were now about sixty butterflies trailing behind me in a menacing cluster. *Crap on a stick.* I was beginning to get the sense that these butterflies were more than just an audience. Was I just being paranoid? It would be understandable after what had happened with Sedgwick.

I turned to address my companions. "I don't know if you're here to watch me meet the unicorn or to impede my progress. Which is it?"

The response was swift and immediate. The butterflies formed a mini tornado. They circled around me like they were preparing to lift me into space with the power of their beating wings. Unlike Daniel's soft white wings, these wings didn't tickle my bare skin. They felt like a thousand tiny needles pricking my skin. My instinct was to start swatting them away, but they were such delicate creatures that I was loath to hurt them. Although I wasn't sure why they were attacking me, I knew that it wasn't in their nature. I needed to defend myself without harming them. I tried to ignore the pain and focus on how to get away. I couldn't reach my wand with the butterflies pressing against me, so I tried to think of a spell that might work without Tiffany's help.

I closed my eyes and focused my will. "Double, double, toil, and trouble/put these butterflies in tiny bubbles."

Tiny pink bubbles appeared all around me. The sensation of pinpricks was quickly replaced by soft gel. I looked to see the butterflies encased in bubbles like bugs in amber. They bounced against me before floating away to safety. I examined my arms and legs for injury. They were red and irritated, but that was the extent of the damage. I continued to watch the butterflies as they disappeared between the trees. The bubbles seemed sturdy enough to contain them for now.

I observed a few bounce off the trunk of a tree without breaking. Good. Whatever they were here for, it wasn't to assist me.

"Keep going, Emma," I told myself. I pictured Daniel's tall frame loping beside me. It was comforting to envision him accompanying me on this journey. Just because I was alone didn't mean I had to feel that way.

I stopped beside the creek and swirled my hand in the cool water. "I do wish you were here with me, Daniel. Everything seems easier when you're around."

"Will I do?" I glanced up from my crouched position to see Gareth hovering beside me.

"Gareth? How are you here?"

Gareth splayed his hands. "You know I've been working with Lyra to manifest in different places," he said. "This time, instead of trying to imagine a specific place, I simply imagined you." He surveyed the forest. "This is where I ended up and here you are, so I guess it worked."

I stared at my vampire ghost roommate in disbelief. "I just defended myself against an attack by a mass of butterflies. I have a feeling they won't be the last obstacle I overcome before I reach the unicorn."

"Well, I don't know how much good I'll do you," he said, "but I'm here for moral support."

"Thank you, Gareth," I said. "It means a lot to me that you're here."

"If there's one thing I learned since my murder," Gareth began, "it's to expect the unexpected."

I heard the sound of scampering feet, alerting me to the arrival of a woodland creature or two. I looked around the forest floor, searching for my newest companions.

"Did you hear that?" I asked.

"Aye," Gareth said. "Typical sounds for the forest, if I recall."

"Yes, except nothing is typical about this forest," I replied.

"Look, only a squirrel," Gareth said, pointing.

"Only a squirrel?" I repeated. "That's like telling Indiana Jones it's only a snake."

Gareth peered at me. "Indiana who?"

"Never mind." I studied the squirrel, wondering whether sixty squirrel friends would suddenly join it. I shuddered at the thought.

"Is it my imagination, or did that squirrel just grow a wee bit larger?" Gareth queried.

Sure enough, the squirrel was now taller than the berry bush it had been standing beside.

"Oh no," I murmured. Unfortunately for me, the growth spurt continued. I watched as the squirrel grew past the bush completely and its tail grew taller and bushier. Yuck. Their tails gave me the creeps even on a small scale. This was no bueno.

"What do we do?" I asked.

Gareth shrugged. "Gather up acorns and be ready to chuck them?"

I searched the forest floor, but acorns were nowhere to be found. What kind of forest didn't have acorns? Apparently, the magical forest I was now in.

The squirrel's teeth grew larger along with the rest of it, a fact that made me increasingly nervous.

"Should I run?" I didn't think running was the answer, though. At the rate the squirrel was growing, he would over-take me in a few short steps. His dark eye fixed on me and anxiety festered in the pit of my stomach. This squirrel was out to get me.

Gareth lifted a branch. "You have to try. I'll hold it off."

"Gareth, you're holding a whole branch," I said. "That's really good work."

Gareth smiled. "Aye. I'm quite proud." He turned to glare at me. "Now run."

I didn't wait to be told again. I sprinted through the trees, making sure to stay as close to the creek as possible. At least the creek gave me a sense of direction. At some point if I kept going, it would empty out into Swan Lake.

I jumped over bushes and my legs suffered as a result of the thorns and prickly leaves they encountered. Sweat dotted my forehead and my heart pounded. According to my ragged breathing and outrageous heart rate, my body was not at its best. If I lived through this, I was going to have to get my butt into an exercise program. If Daniel was ever going to see me naked, I wanted to look my best.

Gareth appeared next to me, not a ghostly hair out of place.

"What happened to the branch?" I asked, panting heavily.

He gave me an apologetic look. "It broke. That squirrel has some seriously strong teeth."

"I don't know where to run," I said. "Even if I climb a tree, I feel like he'll be able to reach me."

"Aye, he will. I hate to tell you, but he's even bigger now."

Not the news I wanted to hear. I slowed my pace in an effort to conserve energy. I wasn't going to be able to outrun the squirrel or hide from it. I needed to use magic, but I didn't want to hurt the squirrel. As much as I disliked the species, it hadn't done anything to deserve being a part of whatever this was.

"Haven't you learned defensive spells?" Gareth asked. "What about the one you used on Mumford?" Mumford was the goblin that killed Gareth. He attacked me in my office, and I survived thanks to the Blowback spell.

"This is different," I said. "Mumford knew what he was doing, but I don't think the squirrel does."

The sound of bushes being trampled increased my heart rate.

"What does it matter?" Gareth said vehemently. "You hate squirrels."

My legs began to tremble. "I admit that they're not my favorite animal, but it doesn't seem right to hurt him just because I don't like him for some irrational reason." I thought about the butterflies and their protective bubbles. If only there was something I could do like that for the squirrel. Could I form a bubble big enough? It wouldn't work the same for the squirrel because of its size and its inability to fly.

"I know," I exclaimed. I yanked Tiffany from my waistband and pointed her at the oncoming rodent of unusual size. The moment his form came barreling through the trees, I focused my will and said, "Trees stand apart/blow out a dart."

The tranquilizer dart shot from the tip of the wand and landed squarely in the squirrel's chest. I repeated the spell, quickly realizing that more than one tranquilizer dart would be needed to take down a squirrel of this size. I continued to back away from the squirrel as its pace slowed. I could see the tranquilizers taking effect.

"Move faster," Gareth urged. "It's going to fall forward."

I noted the gap between us and realized that Gareth was right. I was directly in the landing strip for the squirrel. As it began to fall forward, I gathered all my energy and sprinted out of bounds. The ground shook beneath my feet as the squirrel landed hard on the forest floor. I glanced over my shoulder to see that he'd returned to his normal size.

"That was good thinking," Gareth said.

"Thanks," I said. I noticed his pale skin suddenly looked even paler. "Are you okay?"

"I feel like I'm being pulled back to the house," he said. "I seem to have overstayed my welcome."

I gave him a grateful smile. "I'm glad you were here, even if it was only briefly."

"I'll be cheering you on from the house," he said. "I expect you back by dinner. Magpie and I will prepare a feast for you."

"I look forward to it." I barely finished the sentence before Gareth disappeared. It felt strange to be alone again in the forest. It suddenly seemed eerily quiet. No birdsong or chatter. While I wanted it to calm me, the silence was ominous.

"Okay, unicorn," I said. "I'm overcoming your obstacles. When am I going to get to meet the horse behind the curtain?" Fine, so the unicorn probably wouldn't understand the *Wizard of Oz* reference, but so what? I had to amuse myself somehow.

I took the lapse in activity as a chance to return to the creek and rinse my face and hands. I should have used more deodorant this morning. The unicorn would likely reject me based on body odor alone.

I kneeled on the creek bed, enjoying the cool touch of the water on my skin. As I leaned forward, movement in the water caught my eye. A ripple where none should have been. What now? Alligators? I backed away a few steps, just enough so that I was a safe distance from the water. A white head crested and I realized with a start that it was a horse's head. Was this in response to my request for the horse behind the curtain? There was no horn, so it couldn't be the unicorn. Or could it?

I stared in wonder as the horse emerged from the water and stood in front of me on the creek bed. It was a magnificent creature with powerful legs and a silky mane.

"Hey there, gorgeous guy," I said. I resisted the urge to approach it, uncertain what to expect.

ANNABEL CHASE

The horse whinnied, beckoning me with its expressive eyes.

"Are you supposed to take me somewhere?" I asked. Maybe I was supposed to ride the horse to meet the unicorn. That seemed plausible.

The horse lowered its head and nudged me with its face.

"Okay, I'm pretty worn out from the oversized squirrel. Maybe I'm meant to ride you." I put my hands on my hips, studying the horse's height. "I'm not exactly nimble. Can you lower yourself so I can try to get on?"

The horse understood. It returned to the creek and waded in until its back was low enough for me to reach. I splashed into the water and climbed on its broad back. Once my bottom settled, I felt...stuck.

"Is this magical glue for my own protection?" I asked.

The horse didn't answer. Instead it began to swim toward the center of the creek.

"Don't tell me there's an underwater kingdom where the unicorn is waiting for me," I said. "I'm not very good at holding my breath." Breathing in general had never been my forte.

The horse sank deeper and the water began to swallow me. Instinctively, I kicked out my legs to swim and realized that they, too, were stuck to the horse. I tried to move my hand but couldn't. My entire body was stuck to the horse—a horse that was about to drown me.

"Help," I called. There was no one to help me. Sedgwick was gone. Gareth was gone. I was alone.

My teeth began to chatter, due to the cold water or fear—I wasn't sure.

"Let me off," I demanded. I ran through a host of spells in my mind, but couldn't think of one to remove myself from a suicidal horse. Lack of spells aside, I was drained from using so much magic in one day. Although I practiced every day, it was always in small doses. I chastised myself for not preparing enough for the summoning. I should have worked harder. Now I was going to die because of my ineptitude.

I glanced around widely for something to grab onto. A vine, a rock. Anything. The creek seemed to hold nothing except water and this maniacal horse. And me, of course.

"Emma, sit tight," a voice called.

I looked upward to see Millie hovering above me on her broomstick.

"Sitting tight is kind of the problem," I gurgled, as water rushed around my head.

Millie pointed her wand at the water and said, "Help Emma find the unicorn we seek/part the waters of this creek."

Like the parting of the Red Sea, the water separated, creating a dry area for the horse and me. I managed to cough out some of the water I'd swallowed. The horse became agitated and tried to dive back into the creek. With each step, however, the water receded.

"Nice try, kelpie," Millie called from above us. "Now release her."

"Kelpie?" I echoed. "How do you know its name?"

"That's not its name," Millie said. "It's the type of super-natural beast that it is. A kelpie. They drag innocent people to the bottom of whatever body of water they're in and devour them."

Yikes. I tried harder to free myself, but it was no use. I was still firmly stuck to the deceptive kelpie.

"I'm glued to it," I said. "How do I cut myself loose?"

"In some cases, people have had to chop off hands and legs in order to free themselves," Millie said.

My chin jerked up. "Are you serious? I can tell you right now that is *not* happening here."

171

The kelpie made another run for the water, but Millie's magic kept us both dry.

"I have an idea," I called, thinking of the squirrel I'd subdued. "Use the tranquilizer dart spell that Ginger taught us. If you put it to sleep, I bet the kelpie loses its power over me."

Millie didn't hesitate. She pointed her wand again and said, "For the sake of Emma Hart/shoot me several darts." Multiple darts flew into the side of the kelpie and it swayed back and forth, fighting the overwhelming desire to fall asleep.

I stroked its soft mane. "Sorry, buddy. Don't crush me when you fall over." I called to Millie. "Put the water back, please. Now."

With a flick of her wand, the creek filled the empty space in the middle. It was just in time as the kelpie toppled over and splashed into the water. In that moment, my body was released from its magical hold. I swam to the side of the creek and crawled to dry land. Millie landed in front of me, remaining atop her broomstick.

"That was a close call," she said.

And the Understatement of the Year Award goes to Millie. Well done.

"What are you doing here?" I asked. "This is dangerous."

"Did you really think I was going to let you take all the credit for getting the horn?" she asked. "I'm a virgin, too, you know."

Spell's bells. Millie was even competitive when it came to virginity.

"Fair enough." I caught my breath and rose to my feet. "Seriously, though. You have no idea what I've been through. This is no place for you."

"Why?" she demanded. "Because I'm a remedial witch and not a fancy sorceress?"

I sighed. "No, Millie. Because you're someone I care about."

Her face fell. "Oh." She eyed me. "Are you sure you don't want me to stay? You look exhausted and I did just save you from a murderous kelpie."

I smiled. "Thank you, I am exhausted and fresh out of magic, but I don't want to risk anyone's safety. Sedgwick was hurt and that was more than enough risk for me. I couldn't bear anyone else getting hurt."

"Fine," Millie huffed. "But I'm telling everyone how I saved you."

I bowed. "Be my guest. Spread the word from the rooftops." I had no qualms about needing the help of my friends. I had no desire to be a lone wolf in this world. It was only because I wanted to keep them safe that I was deter-mined to do this alone.

"Do you want me to give you a lift?" she asked.

"I'd say yes, but I have no idea where I'm going. My instinct told me to follow the creek, but you see where that got me."

Millie's broomstick began to rise. "Whatever your flaws, your instincts have always been good, Emma. You should trust them."

"Wow. Praise from Millie," I said. "Must be the magical influence of the sacred unicorn." I made spooky haunted house noises.

"Very mature," Millie snapped. "I can see why the Angelic Boy Wonder loves you. Not."

Instead of flying straight up above the creek where there were no trees, she threaded her way between the trees with expert precision.

"Show-off," I called after her.

As she attempted to break through the treetops and into

the open sky, enchanted vines reached out and wrapped themselves around the shaft of the broomstick.

"Millie," I yelled, but it was too late.

The vines tugged and shook the broomstick as Millie desperately tried to hold on. I was too far away to help her. Some fancy sorceress I was. She'd saved my life and I was about to reward her by watching her die.

CHAPTER 18

MILLIE NEEDED to use magic to free herself, but with both hands on the broomstick, there was no way she could retrieve her wand without letting go. My energy was far too depleted to do anything. I was barely standing on two feet right now. I almost regretted making Sedgwick leave.

As her grip loosened, I bit back a scream.

One good jerk of the broomstick and Millie was thrown into the treetops. The sound of her body hitting each branch on the way down and landing on the ground with a thump would haunt me in my dreams for years to come. I dragged myself through the woods, where I found Millie's body in a heap at the base of a large oak tree.

"Millie, are you okay?" What a ridiculous question. Of course she wasn't okay.

Millie groaned, but her eyes remained closed. A gentle breeze caressed my skin and an odd sensation urged me to turn around. Behind me, golden light filtered through the trees. and, suddenly, there it was.

The sacred unicorn.

"Are you kidding me?" I couldn't believe my crappy luck.

"Hurry, you must," a familiar voice said. "The wheel of time spins on." Petra's form shimmered in the light.

"I can't hurry now," I said. "Millie needs my help."

"The sacred unicorn has been summoned," she said, "but is not required to stay. Tarry and you will lose your one chance to retrieve the horn."

And our one chance to break the curse. I clutched Millie's hand.

"Leave me." Although her voice was weak, the words were clear.

"No," I said firmly. "I can help you." I didn't possess healing magic, but I didn't have to. If I could get back to the healing plant and return quickly, I could use it to save her.

Petra seemed to read my thoughts. "The light fades as you decide. Choose, you must."

I looked past the Grey sister at the unicorn. The white muscular body and golden horn were mesmerizing. It gazed at me, as though awaiting my decision.

"Go to it," Millie said, her eyes fluttering open and closed. "I'm...fine."

"No, you're not," I said. There was no way she'd be fine without immediate help.

"The town needs this," she whispered.

"And you need to heal," I said. "I won't risk leaving you here."

"I can move. See?" Millie twisted her body slightly and howled in pain. "At least my legs don't hurt. They feel numb."

Spell's bells. A possible spinal injury and internal injuries, too, no doubt. My throat thickened. This was an impossible choice. I stood and faced the unicorn.

"Please wait for me," I called. "I'll be back as quickly as I can. My friend is very hurt. If I don't heal her first, she won't live."

The unicorn continued to stare at me with no response. I whipped toward the Grey sister.

"Can you do anything? Make it stay? Help Millie?"

She wrapped her cloak more tightly around her narrow shoulders. "A mere pawn in this game am I."

"Me too, it seems." I inhaled deeply. Okay, it wasn't an impossible choice. Millie's life was more important than the freedom to leave town. No one would want me to sacrifice one of our own just for the chance to leave Spellbound. At least, I wouldn't.

"Stay still, Millie," I said. *Stay alive.* "I'll be back with the healing plant, I promise." I turned toward the unicorn. "Please wait for me."

I didn't hesitate to see whether it would. There was no time to waste. I gathered what remaining energy I had and ran off into the forest, desperate to find my way back to the plants as quickly as possible. I retraced my steps to the best of my ability. It wasn't easy. There'd been many distractions along the route.

Finally, I recognized the cluster of white birch trees that provided the backdrop to the Grey sisters' earlier performance. I slid on the ground and pulled apart a plant stem, complete with leaves and berries. I only wanted to take what I needed. I didn't dare uproot the whole thing and risk losing it completely.

I placed the plant safely in my cloak pocket and raced back toward Millie and the unicorn. As my feet pounded the earth, I prayed to whatever gods were listening to keep the unicorn there long enough for me to heal Millie.

The wind rushed past my ears and I hiccupped from swallowing too much air as I ran. I stumbled twice, and tripped on a tree stump, narrowly missing a brush with thorns. I tried to imagine what condescending statement Millie would make if she could see me now and the thought spurred me onward. Millie was a pain, but she was our pain, and we didn't want to lose her.

"I'm here," I yelled, as I spotted the fading golden light in the distance.

I surged ahead when I saw Millie still on the ground, unconscious. Dropping beside her, I pulled the plant from my pocket. I squished the berries and poured the juice into her mouth. I rubbed the leaves on her body. I did anything and everything I could think of to heal her broken body.

The unicorn began to walk away.

"No," I cried. I couldn't leave. Not yet. I had to be certain Millie was okay before I chased after the unicorn.

The golden light darkened. Tears streaked my cheeks as I opened Millie's cloak and lifted her shirt in order to rub the leaves on her stomach.

"Stop. That…tickles," Millie said softly and opened her eyes.

"Oh, thank you," I said, and hugged her as gently as I could. Tears dripped from my cheeks to hers.

"Gross," she said, and wiped them away.

I studied her. "How do you feel?"

"Like you mowed me down with a broomstick," she replied. Her voice sounded stronger.

"Can you feel your legs?" I asked.

Millie nodded. "I don't have any pain now either."

Thank goodness. "Can you sit up?"

Millie sat up and smiled. A healthy glow had returned to her skin. "I'm fine, Emma. You need to go."

I craned my neck for any sign of the unicorn. "I think it's gone."

"You're as annoying as I am," Millie snapped. "Since when do you quit? Go after it!"

I inclined my head. "You're sure you're okay?"

"I am." She shoved me hard, a sure sign she was feeling better. "Now go."

I glanced over my shoulder to ask the Grey sister for advice, but she was no longer there. "Wish me luck."

"Luck!" Millie called.

I took a deep breath and sprinted through the clearing, chasing the sliver of golden light that remained.

To my great relief, I found the unicorn by the creek.

"I thought you'd gone," I said, struggling to catch my breath.

I was never going to leave, not once you passed the test.

"Which test?" I asked.

All of them, of course. Healing your friend was the final test.

"I don't understand," I said. "The Grey sister said I only had a small window of time before you left. That if I went to get the healing plant, I wouldn't get back in time."

And which Grey sister was that? The one who lies or the one who tells the truth?

Crap on a stick. I'd been had.

If you had chosen to approach me instead of aiding your friend, I would have disappeared. Thankfully, that is not the choice you made. Well done.

My chest ached. Millie's accident had been a test. Like Sedgwick.

You truly are pure of heart, the unicorn said.

I reached out my hand to stroke its silky mane but snatched my hand back, thinking better of it. "May I?"

The unicorn lowered its head, acquiescing to my request. The white mane was every bit as soft as it appeared. Much better than the kelpie.

Now tell me why you have summoned me here.

"I need your horn, please," I said. "For a spell that breaks a curse—a curse that has imprisoned the residents of this town for far too long." The golden horn was so bright and beautiful, the thought of removing it filled me with nausea.

I see. The unicorn tilted its head. *And how do you intend to remove it?*

"With your permission," I said, "I'd like to try a spell." My magic burned within me, a clear sign that I'd had enough time to restore my strength.

No swords or jagged knives?

"That sounds far too violent for me," I said. "I can barely cut tomatoes without destroying them."

The unicorn gazed at its reflection in the water. *My horn is my most sacred part.*

"And I promise to treat it with the respect it deserves."

I know you will, Emma.

My skin tingled. "You know my name?"

I know everything about you, but that is not the reason you've summoned me now, is it?

"No, it isn't." Inwardly, I cursed. I hated to have answers about my past right in front of me without the ability to access them.

It is time for the spell, Emma. Do what you must. My time here is nearly at an end.

I produced Tiffany from my waistband. Although I didn't need her for the spell, I knew she'd help me focus my magic. I only had one chance to do this right.

"Maybe tilt your horn a little to the left," I said. The unicorn moved slightly. "No, not my left. Your left. That's better." I focused my will and extended my wand toward the horn. "Innocent and pure as the day you were born/harmlessly remove this unicorn's horn."

The golden horn rattled for a moment and I held my breath. Then it slid to the side, a clean break from its head, and toppled toward the ground. I snatched the horn before it hit the ground and instinctively kissed it.

"You look like a beautiful white horse," I said.

White horses do not exist, the unicorn said. *Only grey ones.*

Good to know. I clutched the golden horn to my chest. "Thank you for this. All of Spellbound thanks you. Is there any way I can repay you?"

There is a way for you to help me regain what I have lost.

"Name it."

The healing plant you have in your pocket. Use it on my head.

I scrambled to retrieve the remainder of the plant from my cloak. "The berries and the leaves?"

The unicorn nodded. I rubbed the berry juice on its head, followed by the leaf. A bump formed on its head and my mouth dropped open as a new golden horn slowly grew in its place.

"Spell's bells. It restored your horn," I said in amazement.

It's a powerful healing plant. Keep it and grow more. Consider it my gift to you.

"But you've already given me the best gift of all," I said.

No, the unicorn said. *The horn is for the town. The plant is my gift to you.*

"Thank you so much." I stroked its mane one last time. "I'm so glad I got the chance to meet you."

And I you. Good luck, Emma. May the gods smile upon you.

I sighed happily, the golden horn in my hand. "They already have, my friend. More than I ever deserved."

When I emerged from the forest, it seemed like the entire town was waiting for me. Rows of residents stood on the forest border, watching for any sign of me. I raised the golden horn above my head to let them know of our success. A cheer went up in the crowd. In the sea of bodies, Daniel stood out like a beacon in the night. I rushed toward him and buried my face in his chest. His arms engulfed me and I finally relaxed. I didn't realize how tense I'd actually been until now. Not that I was surprised. The pressure had been almost unbearable.

Daniel released me so that others could congratulate me. Begonia was next in line. She threw her arms around my neck and planted a kiss on my cheek.

"I knew you could do it," she said brightly. "Millie said she saw the unicorn. Was it beautiful?"

"It was," I replied. "And very gracious to boot. How is Millie?" I scanned the crowd, but there was no sign of her.

"Boyd insisted that she go to his office for a thorough examination," Sophie said, elbowing her way in. "She seemed fine, though. She was too happy to tell us about rescuing you from the kelpie."

Laurel slipped her head under my arm. "What else happened? Tell us everything."

"There will be plenty of time for that later," Lady Weatherby said, motioning for everyone to move. "Give Miss Hart space, please."

Since when did Lady Weatherby express empathy for me?

"Let's have a look at this horn, shall we?" the head of the coven said.

I handed her the golden horn and she exhaled softly. "It is a lovely specimen, isn't it? How did you manage? Never mind. We'll hold a coven briefing tomorrow morning. For now, go home and get some rest. You've earned it."

I was oblivious to the hands clapping me on the back as I made my way through the crowd. The moment Lady Weatherby mentioned rest, my body began its slowdown. My legs nearly collapsed under me and I leaned against Daniel for support.

"Would you like me to carry you?" he asked. "If I fly, it will only take a minute to get you home."

Normally I tensed at the mention of flying, but I was too tired to be anxious. "Yes, please."

He scooped me up into his arms and bounded into the air as I waved goodbye to my well-wishers.

Gareth was busy pacing the floor of the house when we arrived. "Thank the devil." He enveloped me in a hug and he nearly felt corporeal. "Dinner is on the table if you're hungry. Or I can make you tea and bring it to your bedroom if you'd rather go to bed."

"Thank you," I said. "You all spoil me."

"Hardly," Daniel said. "You're the one risking life and limb to free us from the curse."

"I'm more tired than hungry," I said. "Would you mind terribly if I went to bed?"

"Not at all," Gareth said. "It will keep for tomorrow."

"Goodnight, you two," I said. "I'll see you tomorrow." Slowly I climbed the stairs to my room, where Sedgwick awaited me.

How are you? he asked.

"Forget me," I said. "How are you?"

Completely healed.

"Thank goodness." I had a lot to be grateful for today. I changed into my pajamas and slipped under the covers. My head didn't manage to hit the pillow before I fell fast asleep.

I awoke to Gareth's concerned face hovering above me. I bolted upright. "What's the matter? Is Magpie okay?"

"It isn't Magpie I'm worried about," the vampire ghost replied. "You never sleep this late."

I stretched my arms above my head. "How late is it?" The sun streamed in behind Sedgwick's perch, so I knew it was still morning.

"Nearly eleven," he said.

ANNABEL CHASE

I shot out of bed. "Eleven? Why didn't anyone wake me? I need to be at the coven for the briefing."

"Relax," Gareth said, placing a ghostly hand on my shoulder. "Lady Weatherby came by earlier to check on you. She said to come along whenever you're able."

"That's very accommodating of her," I said in surprise.

"Enjoy it while you can," Gareth said. "I'm sure she'll be back to her usual self tomorrow."

I showered quickly and ate the hearty breakfast that Gareth had prepared before heading to coven headquarters. Sedgwick accompanied me, wanting to give his account of events. He didn't seem to realize that his account would still need to come from me. My voice was his voice, unless we used the talking familiar spell. Knowing Sedgwick, I figured it was best to let me do the talking.

Key members of the coven were already assembled when I arrived. I got the sense that they'd decided to linger until I appeared. No one wanted to miss what I had to say.

"Do come in, Emma," Professor Holmes said, waving me forward.

I walked into the coven meeting room and took a seat at the table, while Sedgwick used one of the side tables as a perch.

"Good morning, Emma," Meg greeted me. She sat in her usual place between Ginger and Professor Holmes.

"Miss Hart," Lady Weatherby said, sweeping into the room and seating herself at the head of the table. "You're looking well."

"Thanks to a good night's sleep," I said. "Where's the horn?"

"In the coven vault," Ginger said. "We'll keep it there until we're ready to break the curse."

"We still need to figure out exactly how to do that," I said.

"It's only a matter of time now," Lady Weatherby said. "Thanks to you and the other witches."

"Tell me, Emma," Professor Holmes said. "How did you prove yourself worthy of obtaining the horn?"

I recounted yesterday's events, starting with Sedgwick and ending with the horn's regrowth. When I finished, the professor gave me a kindly smile.

"And do you understand *why* you passed these trials?" he asked.

"I think so," I said. "The unicorn explained why it didn't leave when I chose to help Millie."

"Some residents might argue that your decision was a selfish one," Meg said. "That you put the future of an entire town at risk for the sake of one witch."

"I chose to help Millie first because I care about her. She's a member of this coven and like family to me. While I admit that sometimes our actions in support of those we love can have negative consequences for others..." I trailed off, my words echoing in my head.

Professor Holmes frowned. "Emma, is something wrong?"

I sat quietly for a moment, letting the realization sink in. "I need to send a message to Astrid." I shot a quick glance at Sedgwick. "I know what happened to Titus."

The members of the coven exchanged confused glances.

"The elderly satyr from the care home?" Ginger queried.

I nodded somberly. "I know who killed him."

CHAPTER 19

ACCORDING TO SEDGWICK, Astrid and Britta were knee-deep in a situation involving angry goblins and a silver chalice, so I decided to head over on my own. If I could handle the summoning, then I could handle a murder suspect.

I knocked on the door of the red brick house and waited. The door jerked open and a familiar troll looked at me.

"Hello again, David," I said.

The troll cocked his head. "Have we met?"

"Briefly, at the Spellbound Care Home," I said. "The day you moved your father in."

His expression shifted. "Oh, right. I remember now. Come on in. You saw my sons at their level best." He chuckled. "They're a handful, but they're ours."

I stepped inside the entryway. It looked like a typical suburban house busting at the seams with clothes and toys.

"How's your father settling in?" I asked. "It's Duncan, right?"

"Yes, he loves it there. We were fortunate to get him in off the wait list. You never know how long it might take."

"How long had he been on the list?"

David scrunched his face in concentration. "I'd say two years. My youngest had just turned a year old. Our house was chaos at the time." He slicked back his thin hair. "What am I saying? It's still chaos."

"I guess you realized then that your father couldn't live with you," I said. "That had to be tough. Three young kids and an ailing father."

David nodded. "I wanted to create an in-law suite for him, but my wife didn't like that as a long-term solution."

"Why?" I asked.

He blew air from his nostrils. "Because she's a smart troll, and she knew she'd be the one to take care of him most of the time. I'm out of the house a lot and she's home with the boys. My father needs constant attention and we knew it would only grow worse as he aged."

"She does sound smart," I agreed.

The door opened and Vera entered the house wearing knee-high garden boots. "I'm a mess." She stopped short when she saw me. "Oh, hello. I remember you from the care home."

"Nice to see you again," I said. "I've been to the care home a few times since, but haven't run into you."

"David thought it was best to give him space to settle in before we bombarded him with visits," Vera explained.

I gave David a curious look. "You haven't been to visit your father since he moved in?"

Vera laughed. "I know. I thought it was strange too, but it makes sense. It's like dropping the boys at preschool for the first time. You leave them so they settle better."

I studied the troll. "Is that the real reason, David? Or were you avoiding the care home for another reason?"

"I don't know what you mean," he replied.

"You love your wife and your father, don't you, David?" I said. "I bet you'd do anything to make them happy."

He shifted uncomfortably. "I would, same as anyone."

"David's a family man," Vera said proudly. "He'd move mountains for any of us. That's the kind of troll he is."

"Vera," David cautioned. She didn't take the hint.

"It was a miracle that he managed to get his father into the care home," Vera said. "I was at my wit's end. Only the week before, I'd nearly had a breakdown over all the work involved. Of course, I was an equal mess over having Duncan move into the home. I wanted him to be cared for properly, even if we couldn't do it." She rubbed her husband's arm. "David made sure the place was up to snuff."

"He's very devoted," I agreed. "Tell me, David. How many times did you tour the care home? I'm guessing it was twice."

"That's right," Vera interjected. "Once when we put him on the list and the second time wasn't long before a spot opened up. It was serendipity."

Or murder. Same thing.

"When you toured the care home, you didn't sign in as a visitor, did you?" I queried.

David's jaw clenched. "No. I didn't have to."

"Have you ever heard of a potion called Organ Massacre?" I asked.

David's expression hardened. "No, I can't say that I have."

"Yes, you have, dear," Vera corrected him. "We read about it in one of the books Anders brought home from the library, remember? We talked about how painful it probably was and you said you'd rather die from external injuries because it would be quicker."

David's cheek twitched. "Vera, I love you to the moon and back, but you need to stop talking."

She patted him twice on the chest and set about removing her boots. "Sorry, I've been so chatty since Duncan moved out. Release of stress, I suppose."

I focused my attention on David. "Are you going to tell her or shall I?"

Vera glanced from me to her husband. "Tell me what?"

David closed his eyes, surrendering to the truth. "I did move mountains to get my dad into the care home. A mountain called Titus."

Vera frowned. "I don't understand."

"Titus died from a dose of Organ Massacre," I said. "His death allowed Duncan in off the wait list."

Vera's eyes widened as the realization set in. "David, what have you done?" Her voice dropped to a whisper. "You killed Sadie's father?"

Her husband's eyes remained closed, unwilling to look her in the eye. Shame seemed to engulf him.

"I did it for you," he said softly. "And for Dad. Titus didn't deserve that place in the care home. You heard the way Sadie talked about her father at book club. He was a complete waste of space."

Vera stared at him. "But that's not for you to decide. We leave decisions of life and death to the gods."

"You were at the end of your rope," he told his wife. "And Dad needed more help than we could give. I arranged a tour so that I could slip in and give Titus the potion. I told him it was a special brand of moonshine and he gobbled it down." He dragged a hand through his thinning hair. "I only hurried Titus along so that more deserving folks could benefit." His eyes met mine. "What will happen to my father? Will he lose his place in the care home?"

"I doubt it," I said. "Duncan's an innocent party. You, on the other hand…"

His thick shoulders slumped. "I guess you've already sent an owl for the sheriff."

"She's on the way," I said. "You may want to have a word with your sons before she gets here."

189

Vera blinked away tears. "Our poor boys. David, what were you thinking? Now they're going to grow up without a father, the same as Sadie."

"I was thinking how much I love you all," David said. "And I wanted to make life better for everyone."

"I'll wait outside for Sheriff Astrid," I said, and stepped outside to give the family their last few minutes of privacy.

CHAPTER 20

I AWOKE from a power nap to see Begonia puttering around my bedroom.

"Hey there," I said. "Everything okay?"

"Just checking on you," she said. "You've been through a lot the last couple of days. I heard about David Bridge."

"Sad," I said, sitting up and leaning against my pillows. "I know he did it out of love for his family, but it was a bridge too far." I cringed. "Sorry, I wasn't trying to make a joke."

"You're probably still exhausted."

"A power nap will help. Daniel is taking me on an evening picnic, so I wanted to be as bright-eyed as possible."

"That'll be nice and romantic." Begonia came and sat on the edge of my bed. "Emma, there's something I've been meaning to tell you about Markos's party."

I shot her an alarmed look. "Is this about Marcie?"

She waved her hands. "No, no. That was exactly as Dem said." She hesitated. "But I already knew I could trust him before that."

"How?"

She chewed her lip. "Before I saw you at the party, I was

wearing Millie's ideal beauty necklace. I wanted to test it out."

A light bulb went off in my head. "On Demetrius?"

Her cheeks reddened. "I know it's dumb, but I wanted to see if he mistook me for you."

Now it was my turn to blush. "Begonia, you know his feelings for you are genuine."

"I do now. He only saw me when I wore the necklace." She smiled and hugged herself, remembering. "I was so happy and relieved."

"So is that what you wanted to tell me?"

Her blue eyes met mine. "Demetrius didn't mistake me for you, but someone else did."

"Daniel?" That wasn't necessarily a surprise.

"No, Markos."

Oh. "Did he figure out you weren't me?"

"No, I passed him on my way to the bathroom. He only briefly said hello again because I guess he'd already seen you, but I think Beatrice may have noticed something. When I took off the necklace and put it in my pocket, she'd turned around and was watching me."

"Hmm, but she doesn't know what the necklace represents."

"She's in the coven, Emma," Begonia said. "I think all the witches were told about our invented spells."

I brought my knees to my chest. "There's nothing I can do about Markos. He's a grown minotaur and he knows I'm completely devoted to Daniel." Not to mention that I wasn't a fan of Beatrice anyway. It was hard to feel sorry for someone who deliberately subjected me to a nightmare.

"I'm not trying to cause trouble. I just thought you should know," Begonia said. "I don't trust Beatrice. She has shifty eyes."

I laughed. "She really does. She was probably a wererat in a previous life. So where's the necklace now?"

"I gave it back to Millie," she replied. "I shouldn't have used it. I need to trust Demetrius. Like he says, trust is the cornerstone of every relationship."

I arched an eyebrow. "Demetrius told you that?"

She nodded. "He really is the sweetest vampire on the planet. Can you believe he went to all that trouble to narrow down rental spaces for me?"

"I do believe it," I said. "Demetrius is wonderful and so are you." I hugged her. "I'm so fortunate to have both of you in my life."

Begonia cleared her throat. "So now that you were able to summon the unicorn and get the horn, does that mean you don't have to stay a virgin if you don't want to?"

"Begonia!"

"What?" She flashed me an innocent look. "You're a grown witch...sorry, sorceress in a loving, committed relationship with an angel. What's stopping you?"

"Nothing, I guess," I said. "It isn't that I don't want to. Daniel is the sexiest, most desirable..."

Begonia held up a hand. "Okay, let's not get into a competition about whose guy is sexier because we both know I'd win."

"Ooh," Gareth said, materializing in a corner of the room. "Is this a sex-off? If so, I vote for Demetrius."

"What?" I said. "Are you nuts? You've seen Daniel, right? Tall, blond, eyes the color of the sea. Huge white wings."

"And you've seen Demetrius Hunt, right?" Begonia countered. "Dark and dreamy vampire with fangs that make you shiver in a good way."

Gareth gave me a smug look. "What she said."

"Let's agree that they're both extremely sexy and we're the luckiest paranormals in Spellbound," I said.

Begonia smiled. "I can make peace with that."

Later that evening, Daniel and I sat on a blanket on Curse Cliff, enjoying an enchanted picnic. It was the one place we knew we could be outdoors and completely alone since no one else dared to walk on the hallowed ground.

"How are you feeling now that the summoning is over and Titus's murderer has been caught?" He squeezed my tight shoulders. "There's still some tension there."

"You know my shoulders. They're always like tightropes."

He feathered kisses along the curve of my neck. "Let me see if I can help you with that."

I closed my eyes and enjoyed the sensation. "We should probably eat."

He winked. "Spoilsport." He unwrapped a drumstick and handed it to me.

"Deep fried," I said happily. "How did the picnic basket know I needed comfort food?"

"The basket knows all," Daniel said. "That's the whole point of using an enchanted one."

"I'm starving," I said, taking a huge bite of chicken. "I'm still making up for yesterday."

"This is perfect," Daniel said, admiring the twinkling stars above our heads. Then he turned and flashed a grin at me. "And you're not so bad yourself."

When he smiled, it was like the sun shining only for me. I basked in its warm glow and silently thanked the enchantress for my good fortune. I knew others would think I was crazy for showing gratitude, but if she'd never cursed the town, I never would have discovered my origins. And, more importantly, I wouldn't have met my true love. I may have met a nice human man and settled down, raised a couple of delightful children, but I knew in my heart that it wouldn't compare to what I had with the angel beside me. Fallen or not, he'd earned my love and I was only too happy to give it to him.

"Daniel, there's something I've been wanting to say to you," I said. My stomach was twisted into knots. I still couldn't believe what I was about to do.

"What a coincidence," Daniel said. "I've been feeling the same way. With the summoning, you've been so preoccupied... I didn't want to burden you with other thoughts."

"That's very sweet of you," I said, smiling. My thoughts briefly turned to Titus and his selfish ways, and I was so grateful that Daniel was the angel that he was. It seemed a shame that Titus never attempted redemption the way that Daniel had. If he had, maybe his life would have turned out differently.

"What is it you want to say?" Daniel asked.

"You first," I said. In case the conversation didn't go my way, I wanted to be able to exit the situation quickly and gracefully.

He held my hands in his and it was as though I could actually feel the love between us—the energy was palpable. My heart soared and I knew I couldn't wait another second to hear the answer to my question.

"Will you marry me?" The question thundered in my ears.

I stared into his turquoise eyes. He seemed as confused as I was.

His brow furrowed. "Did we both ask the same question at the same time?"

I laughed. "We did."

He hugged me tightly against his broad chest. "So I guess your question is my answer."

"Same goes for you," I replied.

He smoothed back my hair and gazed into my eyes. "Should we answer at the same time, just for fun?"

"On the count of three," I said.

Daniel began to count. "One, two…" He kissed me before he reached three, a long, slow kiss that fed the eternal flame in my heart.

"That's cheating," I said, although my objection was undeniably weak.

He flashed a mischievous grin. "Should we try again?"

I knew him too well. He was going to kiss me on three every time. "You're a scoundrel."

"Not anymore, Emma. Not since the day I carried you across the border. That was the day my true redemption began."

I threw my arms around his neck and kissed him again. Finally, there would be a wedding in Spellbound.

And, this time, it was going to be mine.

* * *

THANK YOU FOR READING

I hope you enjoyed **A Drop in the Potion**! If so, please help other readers find the series ~

1. Write a review and post it on Amazon.

2. Sign up for my new releases via e-mail here http://eepurl.com/ctYNzf or like me on Facebook so you can find out about the next book before it's even available.

3. You can buy **Hemlocked and Loaded**, the 9th book in the *Spellbound* series, here.

4. Check out my new series:

Starry Hollow Witches

Magic & Murder, Book 1

Magic & Mystery, Book 2

Magic & Mischief, Book 3

88386954R00115